CETUS WEDGE

a Charlemagne file by

K.A. Bachus

Published in Bangor, Maine, United States of America
Contact the publisher at info@charlemagnefiles.com

Visit: https://www.charlemagnefiles.com

Cover by Marigold Faith

CHARLEMAGNE FILE TIMELINES

Short Story Collection
A Lighter Shade of Night,
mid 60s to early 70s

Novels
Trinity Icon, early 70s
Cetus Wedge, early 80s
Brevet Wedge, nine months later
Lion Tamer, five months later
State of Nature, early 90s
Vory, a year later
Swallow, five weeks later
Quiet Move, late 90s
Goat Rope, 1999

CONTENTS

PROLOGUE

Disaster hung like a bottomland mist over the rented two-bedroom townhouse at the end of a city cul-de-sac. It hung down; it rose from the ground; it inhabited each room. It dripped from the mauve and teal Christmas wreath on the front door, making "Merry Christmas" a mournful greeting.

Mick and Stain sat in an old Buick across the street.

"What are you gonna do with your share, Mick?"

"I ain't fuckin' earned it yet so shut up about it. Just get ready." Mick tightened his ponytail by dividing it behind his head and pulling the two halves in opposite directions.

"Don't wave your arms around like that, Mick. Somebody'll notice. I'm gonna have a real blowout with my share. Party time!" Stain opened and spun the cylinder of the .357 revolver in his lap.

"There ain't nobody here to notice us. The targets ain't here neither, so don't go countin' all them chickens before they're even laid, man. And quit playin' with that piece before you blow your nuts off and then I gotta drive."

"Here comes somebody." Stain closed the cylinder.

A blue and silver minivan pulled up in front of the townhouse. A woman got out, opened the side door, and unlatched a toddler from a child seat. The child was in a bad mood. He whined and kicked her once, then settled into a whimper as she carried him inside.

"Now?" asked Stain. The townhouse front door was open.

"Wait," said Mick.

"I don't know if I can shoot no baby, Mick."

"I'll worry about that. You take care of her."

"I don't know."

"You don't gotta know. You just gotta do. That's the job. Think about the money and just do it."

The woman came back outside. She had brown hair, curly, shoulder-length, blowing wild in the cold wind. She pushed it out of her face, took some grocery bags out of the car, and went into the house. The front door was still open.

"Let's go," said Stain.

"Not yet."

The woman came back to her car a second time. She wore faded blue jeans and white walking shoes that absorbed the better part of a mud puddle as she stepped off the curb. She shook her foot like a kitten. One, two, mud is distasteful. She took the last of the groceries out of the car and slammed the car door. The heavy bags made her waddle a bit as she walked to the house.

"Okay. Come on. Let's do it." Mick opened his car door and stood in the street.

Stain pulled back the hammer on his revolver. He held it in his right hand and reached for his door handle with the left.

"Shit." Mick sat down again and closed his door, hunching down in his seat, trying to be inconspicuous.

Stain turned around. A black car pulled into the cul-de-sac. It was a Mercedes. Fan-cee. It parked behind the mini-van. Three men got out, real dudes, suits and all, two blonds, one with dark hair. They all looked at Stain and Mick, then two of them followed the woman into her house. The one that was left stood on the curb to stare at them.

"I don't like this, Mick. That guy gives me the creeps. He ain't natural. He ain't real."

"He is too natural, Stain. He's a real, natural killer. I seen that look before, man. He's way out there, and we're gettin' the fuck outta here. Drive, man."

Stain started the car and reversed it all the way back out of the cul-de-sac. The man watched them go, then turned and walked into the woman's house.

ONE

My lawyer said I would be acquitted, and I was. That left resigning as the only honorable course, and I took it.

By accident, I met a gunship driver who had been in my pilot training class. He was still flying. I talked to him at a motel coffee shop and pretended I was in town on business like he was. I said I was looking for something better than I was in, not saying that what I was in was a load of the deepest kimchee, what with my unemployment run out, a new baby at home, and a wife who wouldn't even let me back in for my toothbrush last night.

He asked was I current. No. Was I the guy who…? Yes. He took a step backward. I might be contagious. What else had I flown? How long? How many hours? Told him all that. Could I get checked out again? Sure.

He said he knew some people and he'd put a word in for me. I wondered what kind of people he knew. Drop in the night special ops types, the kinds that fly unsafe airplanes into unsafe airspace under unsafe conditions. I got a real estate license while I waited. Didn't make a dime at it.

When the call came and there was no flying in it, I took it anyway because I'm not stupid. I know I'm not likely to fly again and, in the meantime, I've become attached to eating. It's my favorite hobby next to martial arts, and both joys cost money. Besides, Sally said something along the lines of Don't come back till you have a job, and even then, I went through training without her. After graduation, they put me behind a desk like some fucking shoe clerk.

My apologies to any ladies who may read this someday. But then, if you're cleared for WEDGE material, you've seen a lot worse so what the hell.

I kicked and screamed and they sent me upstairs to The Section. I was happy, apprenticed to number fifty-nine of a sixty-man unit. I saw some action at the lowest levels. Sally came to live with me and brought the baby.

I had just come back from a great success in Honduras, not even a reprimand for a change, and things were noisy in the ops room, with congratulations and explanations fly-ing—within strict limits of need to know, of course. It was a Saturday night three days before Christmas. There was some cheer being passed around. I had some, and then some more, and developed a need for peace and coffee. These were in the hall, which was usually deserted because a lot of guys were convinced the coffee machine was just a home for bugs, the kinds that listen, that is, but I'm pretty sure it harbored a few of the other kind, too.

I was surprised to see a round, bald man pressing buttons randomly until the machine relented, dropped a cup, filled it halfway, then spat the rest out at him. He swore at it, took the cup, and looked at me.

"Merry Christmas, Bear."

I winced at the nickname. "Merry Christmas." I resisted the urge to say sir. I'm a civilian now.

"You don't like the name, eh? The Woman says she dubbed you that because your eyes are like a teddy bear's. Your record's more like a grizzly's, though."

The Woman was the only one in The Section. She wouldn't take a nickname, silly tradition she said, nor did she have a special ops coin. Too macho she said, but she gave nicknames to everybody else and never refused a drink when somebody forgot his coin and had to buy the bar. We called her The Woman behind her back. And if you believe that, you don't know us at all. This guy was a higher-up. It was good to know they called her that, too.

"Why don't you get yourself a cup of this..." He took a sip and scowled. "This is vile. They told me you drink this stuff, but I thought it must have been improved. It's still awful. Get some if you must and come to my office."

I fought the machine and won, stepping aside right before it spat at me, so it missed. Then I followed Buddy to his office. Long ago when he was a young hotshot agent there must have been meaning in the name, but now it was hard to think of the number two man in the organization and the number one man in everybody's estimation (everybody with any sense, that is), as a Buddy.

"What do you think of Jello?" he asked when we were in his office.

"I...."

"He's an idiot."

I kept my mouth shut. Jello was Chief of Section, Buddy's boss.

"How do you think he got his name?" he asked.

"He...."

"He melts in any degree of heat," said Buddy. "I know you heard it's because his face twitches like a bowl of gelatin or some similar nonsense that he's been putting out, but I know better. I was there when he got the name. He was an idiot then, too. He had WEDGE before me and got a lot of the wrong people killed, nearly including his own team. Fred Dolnikov was our boss at the time. He said to me, 'Buddy, I'm gonna save Jello's life. Hope it doesn't cost you yours. See if you can get a handle on these guys. If they live, they're going to be the best.' Sit down, Bear. Oh. Sorry! I won't use that name."

He waddled behind his desk and was silent for a minute as he sifted through piles of paper looking for something. "Sit down," he said again without looking up.

I obeyed. I sat in a worn easy chair in front of the desk, facing sideways toward the door. I looked around quickly. The man was the equivalent of a general and I was in his office. Even in the Air Force I never had this kind of attention without being in trouble, and here I was, the lowest, newest covert ops officer, in the same room with the man at the top, the man who handled WEDGE operations. I did not even know what WEDGE was, though I was getting an inkling. I knew that at some altitude far above my pay grade, we stopped using in-country operatives and began paying mercenaries and assassins. I also knew that way up in the ionosphere these mercenaries and assassins gave way to what were called specialists.

Buddy's was a pretty typical high-ranker's office, mahogany desk, stuffed chairs, credenzas, bookshelves, and all that. The picture behind his desk was unusual, though, not just because any pictures drove the counterintelligence sweepers crazy—one more place to hide things—but also because it was a picture of a window. No kidding. There was a sash, panes, sill and all, with a view of a park beyond it, complete with joggers and children, and even a mugging going on beneath the trees in the distance. There was a real curtain rod above it, and real curtains hung on either side. CI must have hated it.

"You like my picture?" asked Buddy.

"It's...."

"It's my snorkel, my ventilation, a lifeline to the surface world. I gotta have a window."

Strange statement from what amounted to a senior citizen in a world completely devoid of windows. The Section occupies an inner rectangle of corridors and offices, with a walk-in vault at its center for documents. It is surrounded by an outer rectangle of more offices, themselves without windows. The only windows in the entire building are on either side of the glass doors at the entrance to the lobby downstairs.

"No, really," he insisted, "what do you think about it?"

"I think I would be uncomfortable with my back to it."

He narrowed his eyes at me, which was not easy to do with eyes that bulge like that. "How long have you been here?" he asked.

"Six months."

There was an awkward pause as he stared at me and I stared back. "So soon," he muttered, then looked down at the paper he had in his hand. "Here's your game name. Stephen Donovan. Good Irish name. It has an honorable history in this business."

"I ain't Irish. I'm from Texas."

"Too bad. The computer calls the shots. You're Steve Donovan. This operation is designator NT, operation name CETUS, account WEDGE. I'm Frank Cardova, by the way. Call me Frank. Here's your legend." He handed me the computer-generated history of Steve Donovan.

I only glanced at it. I was trying to figure out how to explain this to Sally. Everything was classified, even the parts I understood, which were few. *Honey, I can't be here for Christmas because I'm needed for something important. They'll probably*

paint circles on my chest and call me Bull's Eye. Maybe I'm the
test dummy for a new weapon.

"Relax, Steve," said Buddy. "This is a promotion."

Was I that transparent or was Buddy's mind-reading the result of experience?

He started talking. "No doubt you know that WEDGE is our computer designation for the specialist team known to the rest of the covert world as Charlemagne. Have you heard of them?"

I shook my head.

He whistled. "You do know what a specialist is?"

"Not really."

"A babysitter?"

I shook my head.

He whistled again and closed the curtains over his picture. The room seemed darker. He came around his desk and sat in the easy chair across from me, his back to the door. He put one pudgy hand on each knee and took a full minute to think before he began.

"Steve, you are just now making the transition from a bubble cockpit to these concrete hallways. You're learning fast. After twenty-five years, I still have not adjusted to my room without windows. But there are men so immersed in the muck of our world—and you will learn how deep that is —they are so sucked down into it that they inhabit rooms that not only don't have windows but there are no doors, either. They're not just locked in, they're walled in. These are specialists, my boy. They take incredible risks and they do the impossible."

"Why?" I asked. "Do they do it for money?"

"They do it for buckets of money. Fantastic sums. But money is only another tool. Survival is their constant business."

"How, exactly are they different from regular mercenaries?"

"Besides the difference in price, they are far more effective. With a good babysitter, everything a specialist does is neat and tidy. There are NO repercussions."

"Babysitter?"

He bit his lower lip and thrust out his top chin. "You know that when you have to handle toxic chemicals, you're always careful to put on gloves, right? Well, a babysitter is like a pair of good heavy-duty gloves that the hierarchy puts on when national security requires them to use a specialist."

"And if there's a slip?"

"The glove takes the burn." He smiled. "I am about to be promoted. As Charlemagne's babysitter, I claim the right to choose my successor, and I have chosen you. Congratulations."

"What if I screw up?"

"You won't."

"What if I do?" I insisted.

The smile went away. "Oh, there's no doubt you'll burn, but I understand you're used to that."

TWO

I had a few questions. Closest to my heart: Why Me?

Frank got up, picked up the paper coffee cup on his desk, took a sip, and gagged. I had not touched mine, and now it was too cold anyway. Frank threw his, full, into a trashcan. It spattered across the wall on its way down.

"What is the first rule of deception, Steve?"

"Lead, don't feed."

"Very good. The best deceptions are thought of by the deceived. Now tell me the first rule of intelligence."

"Verify."

"Why?"

"Because of the first rule of deception."

"I find," said Frank with a sigh, "that I become more perspi... more perce... more brilliant with age. Of course, you know those two rules by heart. So does everybody else in The Section. The difference is that you live them. You have a pronounced problem following any other rules, my budding babysitter, Mr. Steve Donovan, but your performance so far shows a deep understanding of the principles of intelligence." He shook his round, nearly hairless head sadly. "Unfortunately, no one else does, least of all Jello, which is why we are here. A bureaucracy is like a septic tank, you see. The lightest material floats to the top, while the heavyweights decompose at the bottom. I think I'll stir the soup some and see what happens."

Frank hitched his belt up around his middle, clasped his hands behind his back, and began to pace, slowly, throwing his head up periodically when searching for a word.

"Let me see," he said. "About eight months ago, Jello sent me on a prodi... a ponder... a big wild goose chase. Something, somewhere, was going down and Charlemagne was needed and would I go get them please, verification would be forthcoming. I knew better, but orders are orders. I made contact and offered them the commission. They asked for verification, of course."

"So they don't end up killing somebody innocent?" I asked.

He stopped abruptly and tilted his head in my direction. "Nobody in our little windowless world is innocent, dear boy. Charlemagne wants verification so they are not deceived. It would be so easy for the Other Side to set somebody up and have us pay for it, and it would be just like them, too. They're such cheapskates. Where was I?"

"Verification."

"Oh yes." He started pacing again. "I told them I didn't have it, that my boss had it, and I would provide it before the start of the operation. They laughed. Then they walked out. I haven't been able to make contact with them since. That particular operation was a cata... a casta... a disaster. So was another one that came up in September. We could not find Charlemagne when we needed them. That was enough for the powers above me. I've already been told Jello is out and I'm in. Last week he went off on a pet project he thinks is going to get him promoted. When he comes back, he enters The Section History Book and I become Chief."

He stopped pacing and leaned toward me, hands on his desk. "The problem is, I can't do that job and this one at the same time. Who's to babysit Charlemagne? I think you're the best choice, the only choice. They'll eat you alive at first, of course, because you're so ignorant. What can you expect? But you're a natural intelligence officer, you speak German, you have me to train you—a considerable advantage—and you're a scrapper. I think you will survive. Close your mouth, Steve. It makes you look even more ignorant than we already know you are."

He stared at me with bulging eyes, like a frog deciding, is it dust or insect?

"I assume from what I know of you that you want the empl... the occu... the job. Stop me before I go any further if that's not the case." He tilted his head. "What's that?"

"I want the job," I said aloud.

"Good. Good. Be sure you have some reason ready that they'll accept. They will press you hard to find all your personal buttons. You won't want to give them too many of the real ones."

"Them?"

"Charlemagne."

Frank sat down again, this time behind his desk. Now he was the boss and I the subordinate, he the teacher, I the student. I listened, but without the real thing, without the actual people in front of me, I found it hard to remember more than the bald descriptions of the men he had known for more than fifteen years.

"I'll start with Sobieski," began Frank. "His is the famous name. His father was a solo specialist before him, one of the best, if not the best. My old boss, Fred Dolnikov, was his babysitter. The elder Sobieski died when this one was a youngster. I don't know how he took up with Charlemagne, but he's their weapons man, an explosives expert of the first rate, a fair marksman for a specialist, which means he's a helluva lot better than you or I will ever be but not the best in the biz as they say.

"He is considered the best at unarmed fighting, though. Like you, he has black belts in various styles. Also like you, he's medium to short, medium build, brown hair, but his is a little lighter than yours, almost blond. He has the prominent Slavic brow ridge over very, very light grey eyes, so light sometimes they seem colorless. He is missing the last two fingers of his right hand. He's almost forty by now."

"Forty?"

"Yes. Don't you start thinking that's old, Steve. With any luck, you'll get there yourself some not very far away day. Don't think these guys look like me, either." He patted his middle. "If anything, I've seen them become faster over the years. They had to, to survive this long.

"Where was I? That's right, Sobieski. Character? Hard to tell. I could sum the other two up pretty well, but this one is difficult. He seems to like Americans and everything American, whereas the others don't. His whole life is a long survival story, so he's more like a machine in some respects. He is quiet and difficult to know. I've never heard him say much and have always depended on Mack to keep him from killing me outright. The others call him Vasily and that's the name on his passport. He carries an Austrian passport, always in his real name, that lists him as a Polish refugee. His mother was Ukrainian, or so I understand.

"The Frenchman, on the other hand, never uses the same name twice, though his passport is always French. They call him Louis, pronounced the French way, but I have no way of knowing if that is his real name. He's fairly tall, about six-two, early forties, dark hair and eyes, slim build. He's the marksman. I don't know of anybody, east or west, who can beat him. He also picks locks and sets up pretty incredible surveillance. This guy is truly dangerous, vola... explo... unstable. He can be cruel, too. But he tells some pretty good jokes."

Frank leaned forward, put his arms on his desk, and played with a pencil for a minute before going on.

"The one who scares the bejesus out of most people, and I think with good reason—the longer I know him, the more reason I see—is Mack. I suppose you might call him the leader of the team. The others defer to him, anyway. While the Frenchman may be slightly insane, it's a human insanity, recognizable, almost familiar. Mack is perfectly sane. His judgment is flawless. If there is any question at all, any fork in the road, he will take the secure turn, even if it costs an extra life." Frank broke his pencil. "It is important never to be a security risk in Mack's eyes."

So far, I could see the wisdom in this.

He continued, "When I talk about him to other people, I call him Mack, because he uses a knife when silence is important. To his face, I say 'Sir.' The other two call him Misha. I don't know why, and frankly, I am less tempted to be curious every time we go out. From his accent, I gather that he is Austrian, though even for me, his accent holds more information than I can grasp. There is an odd quality to it that I can't figure out. He uses Austrian, German, and Swiss passports in various names."

There was a long pause.

"What does he look like?" I asked finally.

Frank played with his pencil pieces a little while longer. He shrugged. "Blond, very blue eyes, about forty. A little taller than you are, I suppose." He looked across the desk at me. "You'll know him the minute you meet him. He is unmistakable. He reads minds, too, by the way. It can become...."

He did not finish his thought. He did not even try leafing through the mental thesaurus he carried in his brain. He let the sentence, the topic, the training session, and the mission briefing, die on the spot.

"And CETUS?" I asked when he let go of his pencil pieces.

He looked up at me again. "The operation? It isn't properly called an operation, but I had the computer name it so we would have some way to charge expenses. I told you I haven't been able to contact them for eight months, didn't I?"

I nodded.

He stood up, took a paper from a stack on the left side of his desk, and handed it to me. "Imagine my surprise, then, when I saw this today. I hope you have a warm suit in that bag you brought back from Honduras. We'll take separate flights. Yours leaves first."

I was actually holding a WEDGE document. Since then, this has become routine, but at the time it was not just new, it was a revolution in my career, a coup d'état in a country heavily dominated by mercilessly suppressed rebellion. After Frank's weak description of Mack, I dimly understood the danger, but it could not dampen the thrill that went through me when I held that standard form message peppered with all the usual, mundane TSECRET/WNINTEL/NOCONTRACT/SPECAT caveats and stamped at the top with the rare and almost magical word: WEDGE. I managed to read it; I devoured it, every computer jot, even the date-time group. It was from the FBI in Chicago. I was surprised. It had always been my impression that we did not speak, except during summits at the highest levels. Some people I knew ranked the FBI up there with the Other Side on their personal enemies list.

"Who is Eben Jared?" I asked. "Or, who was he?"

"None other than the Other Side's top solo specialist." Frank rubbed his hands together. "Eben Jared did his apprenticeship with the IRA, then attended all the top KGB schools for the particularly nasty, and finally set up on his own, freelance. He always gave them special rates. He was very, very good."

"But he's dead," I said. "So what's one more dead bad guy? Chalk one up for our side."

Frank whistled. "You are a cold one. Wet operations like this are not welcome in this country without our knowing about them. Who commissioned it? It is our job to find out."

"Not to mention who killed him," I said. I gave back the message and stood up, ready to go.

"Oh, we know who killed him," said Frank.

"I didn't see any mention."

"It's right here." Frank stabbed at a line of numbers with a fat index finger. The nail was bitten. The numbers meant nothing to me.

"Right here," Frank insisted. "The number of the ballistics match. That's Mack's gun."

I called Sally from the airport. She hung up on me.

THREE

"Can I help you?"

That's what she said, not what she wanted to do. Chicago's O'Hare Airport was largely deserted, of car rental companies at least. This little shrew had the only open counter.

I looked around. A man in front of me leaned on the counter, staring at her, his right hand clenched in a fist.

"Me?" I asked the woman. I don't butt in.

"Yeah, you." She said it to some point over my shoulder. She chewed gum noisily, like the desk clerk behind the counter in support section who issued my new shoes. He made me sign a form for the license, credit card, and passport that established my game name. He put a big X by the spot so I wouldn't miss it. I signed 'Steve Donovan'. Little things like that upset these bureaucratic types.

"So whaddayoo want?" She cracked her gum.

"Guess."

"We only got luxury cars left."

I did not want a conspicuous car. I looked around. Nobody else was open.

"It'll have to do," I said.

"It's a hundred and twenty-five bucks a day," she said, trying to talk me out of it.

The man in front of me pounded his fist on the counter. "You told me you didn't have any cars at all left."

"You don't want no luxury car." She popped the gum at him. It was not a pretty sight.

"I do so want a luxury car, you...." He closed his mouth with effort, but I didn't have any trouble figuring out the word he wanted to use.

With a noisy sigh, the woman drew a form from under the counter in slow motion. "Driver's license," she said to no one in particular.

The man produced an Iowa license from a slim black wallet and gave me an apologetic smile for interrupting.

I looked at him. He was young, blond, and not particularly well dressed. It was the smile that caught my attention. There was something hard in it, like a penny in a cake, only I couldn't be sure what value to place on the penny. I was probably making it up, fooling myself in the spirit of deception. Never give anything away, the schoolhouse had taught me, even a lie. Lies are better believed when the target makes them up. Just give him the ingredients. Here I was concocting nonsense like a fool.

I decided I was imagining the penny. This guy was all cake. The woman was right; he couldn't afford the car he was renting. He was a middle-class junior manager of some kind, probably a salesman on commission who would have to land a big one by Christmas just to pay for the car.

"You're twenty-four," the woman said to his license.

"You get a gold star for arithmetic," he replied.

Maybe there's a walnut shell or two in this cake.

"You can't rent one of our cars," the woman told him triumphantly.

"Why not?"

"Our insurance starts at twenty-five."

"I thought twenty-three was the standard."

"Ours starts at twenty-five."

"I have my own insurance."

"Company policy. I don't make the rules."

"No. But you revel in them."

If that got a sneer, I couldn't see it. Perpetual boredom and all that jaw work on the gum masked her expression as she held her hand out to me and said, "License."

I hesitated. Another counter was opening. The Iowan walked over there. "Sure," said the competitor, "we have midsized cars."

I defected without remorse, fell in behind the man from Iowa, and watched him fill out the form. He opened his wallet and pulled out a credit card with numbers so scraped and worn I could not read them. A picture fell out from behind the card. I picked it up from the floor and had a good look at it before giving it to him. An older couple, salt of the earth and apple pie, standing smiling in the snow in front of a shiny green and yellow tractor. There was a large red bow on the tractor's grill. The man in the picture held up a set of keys.

The woman behind this counter also held a set of keys. "Here you go, Mr. Taylor," she said as she handed them over. "It's a blue Ford Taurus, spot one four seven. There is a shuttle to the lot every ten minutes from just outside the door."

Though we did not take the same shuttle, I saw the Taurus pull out of the lot just ahead of me twenty minutes later. I saw it again as I took the exit for the Dan Ryan Expressway and headed south. And there it was in the underground lot at the hotel Frank told me to use. At the reception desk, I stood in line behind Charles Taylor of Iowa once more.

"Maybe it's under the name Peter Baker," he was saying to the reception clerk. "I'm a substitute for him. Peter Baker. From John Deere. Anything?"

"No, sir, I'm afraid...." The man studied a computer screen and clicked the keyboard a couple of times to make it look good.

"Any vacancies?" Taylor's expression was weary, his voice desperate.

"No. I'm afraid... wait, yes... yes, I do. We've had a couple of cancellations." He handed both of us registration cards to fill out.

"We're neighbors!" said Taylor when we were given the keys to rooms 632 and 634. "I'm Charlie Taylor." He held out his hand.

"Steve Donovan."

"How about a drink?" said Taylor. "There were no cars and no rooms until you showed up. You must be lucky. I'll need you around if there are any girls in the bar. I'll buy." He spoke quickly for a farm boy. "Are you married?" He asked it as we stepped out of the elevator but didn't wait for an answer. "You look married. Then again, I guess not. No ring. That's good. Neither am I. I'll meet you in the bar in fifteen minutes."

I spent most of that fifteen minutes studying my left hand. Of course, there was no ring. Marriage was not in Steve Donovan's legend. But the mark of the class-B bachelor was missing, too, because I never wore my wedding ring. It was dangerous in the cockpit and my wife had long ago locked it up to keep me from losing it. I pondered my unmarked hand for some time. This was such a small thing, insignificant, infinitesimal, as Frank would try to say, but Charlie's word 'lucky' ran through my brain again and again. My life had been a continual dogfight for so long that I was not accustomed to friendly airspace.

Charlie drank his scotch straight. I had mine watered down because I had to meet Frank at the morgue in just over an hour.

"What brings you to Chicago, Steve?"

I'm learning how to babysit a team of specialists.

Steve Donovan's half-page computer story did not satisfy the boy from Iowa, so I found myself filling in the gaps to defend against Charlie's carpet bombing of questions. I was pretty proud of myself, sticking to First Principles, Things I Know, and making them Steve's. I saw no reason why an

FAA inspector should not have been an Air Force pilot in his previous life.

"What did you fly?"

I shrugged. "F-15s." It came out so smoothly, so convincingly, because it was true.

Charlie's blue eyes opened wide. "Really?" he said, with proper respect. "Did you ever shoot anybody down?"

Shit.

I suffered a century in the minute that it took me to come up with an answer. I finished my drink and chewed a piece of ice to buy time. "Air-to-air combat is a discipline, you see. Um… Orders are important, ah and ah, followed. Mostly."

Lame, I know.

Charlie nodded seriously, impressed by my sagacity. I felt my stomach turn.

"What's it feel like to fly a jet like that?" he asked.

"One of the best things about it is that it's the ultimate big picture," I said. "Before the gear is up, everything on the ground is small, smaller. Eventually, every stupid thing and every ugly thing is gone. What's left is perfect: perfect sea, perfect clouds, even perfect cities with straight, parallel streets and beautiful lights."

I sucked on another ice cube. Charlie didn't say anything.

"Another aspect of flying," I said when the ice was gone, "is that for me anyway, it's so natural. The airplane is part of me. Moving is like breathing—at Mach. There's life, freedom, power, joy, woven into a tendon that runs all through my body and out through the stick and back again at every response."

"You must miss it," Charlie said after a long pause.

I was looking at my empty glass. "Yes," I nodded. "Ah, No! I mean, I miss the F-15, of course, but I'm still flying BA-76s for the FAA." *Did I cover that?* I could not remember if I had. Who the hell programmed the computer to put that airplane in Donovan's legend? I've never been in a BA-76. I'm not even sure I know what one looks like.

I told him I had to meet somebody and said so long before he could start another friendly inquisition. There are so many disgusting little details on the ground, like having to lie to likable people.

In the underground lot, I tripped over a bum who sat leaning against a pillar near my car. He was filthy, reeking, and drunk. In his fist, he held the neck of an open bottle wrapped in a brown paper bag. He wore one cracked sunglass lens; the other side of the frame was empty. It made him look like a pirate. Spilled booze, or something worse, glistened wetly on his greasy, grey-streaked beard. I found myself despising him. A ragged piece of cardboard taped to a box next to him said *homlees.* There were some coins in the box. I did not add to them.

"Bastard!" He screamed at me as I unlocked my car.

FOUR

"How do you do? I'm Nelson Hunsecker. FBI."

He looked like a banker: three-piece suit, greying temples, smug like a vault. He ignored my boss and held his hand out to me.

I shook it saying, "Steve Donovan," and introduced Buddy as "my boss, Frank Cardova."

Hunsecker had a subordinate with him that he did not introduce. The subordinate seemed vaguely familiar.

We were standing in a small, private room at the morgue. A dozen body-sized drawers were stacked in three rows of four along one wall. A small desk stood in the opposite corner. On the desk were a phone and a phone book open to a Yellow Pages listing of funeral directors. Otherwise, the room was empty, except for the echo of our voices and the shuffle and click of our footsteps on the flecked linoleum floor. Cold does not affect me, but I felt it this time, though I did not know if the room was cold, or if I only thought it was.

"I want you to know that we are at your disposal," said Hunsecker. "Anything you need, any support at all, just say the word." The man was still talking to me.

Frank answered him. "Thank you. Can we get down to business? Where's Jared?"

"Right here." It was the subordinate who answered and led us to the wall of drawers.

This guy was younger than Hunsecker, short, muscular, and black, with an enormous head and heavy features. Uncomfortably familiar. He opened the first drawer on the left in the upper row. We crowded around the body of a red-haired man, about forty years old, apparently undamaged.

"You verified the ballistic match?" Frank was asking Hunsecker.

"Twice." It was the subordinate who spoke.

"Mack's gun." Frank reminded me.

"Where did you find the body?" he asked Hunsecker.

The younger man answered again. "In an apartment on the South Side. I'll take you there tomorrow."

"Who are you?" asked Frank.

"Sorry. I'm Jay Turner."

I wracked my brain but the name didn't mean anything to me.

"Jay here is a very fine member of our anti-terror squad," said Hunsecker.

Frank ignored him and asked Turner, "Time?"

"Eleven-thirty this, excuse me, Saturday, morning."

"You know exactly?"

"There are witnesses."

"Lovely." Frank did a mental calculation. "You must have been on the scene almost immediately. Who notified you?"

"The police."

"How did they know?"

"One of the witnesses kept telling them that the deceased was her husband, named Eben Jared, but he was carrying an Algerian passport in another name. The cops thought that was odd and called us right away."

"Nice to know somebody has a brain," said Frank looking at Hunsecker. To Turner, he said: "One of the witnesses said she was his wife? And the other one?"

"The other is a twelve-year-old girl. Seems to be his daughter."

"Daughter? Named Jared? And his wife called herself Mrs. Eben Jared?"

"Yes." Turner squirmed under the frog stare.

Frank turned to Hunsecker. "How long has the Jared family lived in your fair city, may I inq... ask?"

"Inkask? We don't have that infor...."

"All their lives," interrupted Turner. "The woman and child were both born here. As far as we can tell, they have always resided here."

"And at that address?"

"Ten years."

"Ten years? And when did you first learn all of this?" Frank's voice was rising.

"This afternoon."

"Nice work." Hunsecker bestowed a condescending smile on Turner.

"Nice work?" Frank's voice was tinged with hysteria, his face red. The redness spread upward to the bare dome at the top. "Tell me," he said to Turner through clenched teeth. "Tell me that they were an estranged couple and he rarely visited. Tell me she is an inconspicuous, homely little woman who is active in the church down the street. You can tell me this, can't you?"

"I am afraid I cannot." Turner hesitated, embarrassed.

Hunsecker tapped his foot on the linoleum impatiently.

"Actually," Turner managed to say under the heat of Frank's stare, "they were happily married. He lived there for about four months of each year, in total."

"And Mrs. Jared?"

"Reporter for the Daily Proletariat."

"Which is?"

"A rag funded by the Other Side."

Hunsecker interrupted: "Can we get back to the matter at hand? I have a meeting."

"This is the matter at hand," said Frank.

"What is?" Hunsecker gave Frank one of the condescending, patient looks he had been bestowing on his assistant. "Come, come now. We can save our condolences to the widow for some other time. Right now we need to clear this little matter up. She is demanding release of the body and we can't guarantee she won't go to the press behind our backs."

I knew that any minute now, Frank's eyes would pop out of his head and bounce on the linoleum.

"Doesn't it bother you, Hunsecker," Frank said slowly, "that the top solo specialist in the Eastern Block has been living more or less openly in your city for the last ten years, with a woman who holds a position in a KGB propaganda organization, and you only found out about it this afternoon? By God!" Frank lit the afterburner and ran to the desk in the corner. "I'll bet he's in the phone book! How much do you wanna bet he's in the phone book?"

"I don't think…"

"That's obvious." Frank picked up the white pages. "J. J-A. Ah hah! What street is this apartment on, where you found the body?" he asked Turner.

"Edbrooke."

"With an 'e'?"

"Yes."

Frank read the entry, "Jared comma, E period comma, Edbrooke Avenue." He looked up. "He's in the fucking phone book for heaven's sake!"

Hunsecker shrugged. "Yes, but he's dead now."

And then Frank gave up.

"You know, Mr. Hunsecker…." He forced the 'mister' through his teeth. "I don't want to take any more of your valuable time. You're right. We need to release the body as soon as possible, and I'll get right on it, but I think an under-ling will suit my needs just fine." He pointed at Turner. "Is this one any good?"

Hunsecker scratched his chin. "I guess he's all right."

"Then he'll do nicely. Good night, Sir."

Hunsecker started at this dismissal, gave Frank a narrow look, turned on an expensive Italian heel, and left the room.

Frank played connect the dot with his toe on the speck-led floor. "Now then, you've got a lot to tell me," he said.

"Yes, I do," said Turner. "But first, allow me to assure you that we are not fools."

"Try."

"Hunsecker compartmentalized everything. The Daily Proletariat was CI's bailiwick. They noticed Mrs. Jared but had no way to connect the name with our files in Anti-Terror. They cleared her early on because she is a true believer. She is unaware that the paper is KGB-funded, and she still thinks her husband was a salesman. CI has been performing regu-lar semiannual checks on her that, of course, the husband has managed to avoid, but in any case, his face would have meant nothing to them."

"But it meant something to you," I said. "Don't you have watchers at the airport? Wouldn't they have picked him up? I mean, a man with red hair and freckles carrying an Alger-ian passport?"

"Thanks, pal," said Turner. "They did. This morning. They tailed him for twenty minutes and lost him. They're good watchers." He looked at Frank. "When they lost him, I knew we had somebody big in the city."

"Make no mistake, my friend," said Frank. "You had somebody bigger. Let's go on. Give me an outline of the scenario and we'll go back over the details."

"Not here," said the FBI man. "I managed to secure a room here in the building where we can talk. I have already put up other information there. But before we go, I have something else to show you."

Turner walked over to the wall of drawers and pulled open the one next to Jared's.

"Sister-in-law to Jared," he said. "Killed by Jared's gun."

We looked at the waxen face of a beautiful black woman.

Jay opened the next drawer. "Neighbor of the Jareds, across the hall. A part-time whore killed, we believe, a few minutes before Jared. The bullet used was an odd one, a 7.65 French long, which matches number 17665Y on your watch list."

"The Frenchman," Frank told me.

"He is French then?" asked Turner. "I wondered. The report I received was that he was a Cajun and this woman's lover. If he is one of yours, why would he use such a weak charge?"

"Because it's French."

Turner's heavy brow wrinkled.

"If bubblegum were French, he would use it. Don't worry. His accuracy more than makes up for it."

"We noticed." Turner opened the last drawer in the row. "Now we reach the more interesting facts of the case. Those three were on the scene and we had them immediately. But as I investigated the incident and my investigation kept me on the premises here, I noticed some others. I have them all impounded."

We looked at the man in the drawer. He had been badly beaten, but the cause of death was most likely the hole at the top of his nose.

"The weapon is not on any list," said Turner, "but I believe these corpses are connected. This one is Nikolai Kolnichkov, a mid-level spook of the Other Side who, interestingly enough, has been on our missing list for the past six months." He paused. "We are convinced he has been on their missing list, too."

"Your source?" asked Frank.

"I cannot say."

"Verified?"

"No."

"When did he die?"

"About twelve hours before Jared."

"Why was he beaten? To teach or to learn?"

"I am sorry. I do not follow you."

"I like an honest man." Frank smiled. "Was Ivan here neatly pulverized to teach him a lesson or to learn something from him?"

Turner thought for a moment. "I would have to say to learn. Of what use is teaching someone a lesson only to put a bullet in his brain?"

"Bless you, my son."

Turner raised his eyebrows and threw a questioning glance in my direction. I shrugged. I was not quite used to Frank, either.

"And in what caliber did death come to our pickled Russian?" asked Frank.

"Ordinary nine-millimeter parabellum."

"From whence?"

"We think from Austria."

"Interesting. Any ideas on the weapon?"

"Glock 17. Is it one of yours?"

Frank did not answer.

"Is this the last body?" I asked.

"No." Turner closed the drawer. "There are five more."

"Same three guns?"

"In four of them. One of each in three, and an extra French bullet in the fourth."

"And the fifth?" asked Frank.

Turner drew his next breath through his teeth, looked at the floor, and said quietly. "This may not fit. It may be a simple murder, but I don't think so, and I'll tell you why when we're in the secure room. Right now, we'll just take a look at him so we all have a picture of what we're talking about."

He opened a lower drawer. An older man lay there, muscular and tanned. His hair was cut short, yet one sideburn ended in a Hasidic lock. "I made sure they left one sidelock," said Turner, "to give you an idea of how we found him. It is glued to his face. We found him in a complete Hasidic costume, all of it fake but well used."

"So you think he was a spook dressed up to look like a Hasid?" asked Frank.

I could not resist. "Or maybe," I said, "it's Halloween at the Chicago FBI and he was looking for a treat."

As they say, if looks could kill.

FIVE

"That remark was unnecessary and tasteless," Turner said to me when we got to his secure room, "but I will consider the source."

"Anybody with half a brain should be able to recognize a joke."

"Anyone without a brain should recognize a stupid one."

"Your problem is you take yourself too seriously," I said.

"I do not require advice from an adolescent flyboy."

"Boys! Boys!" Frank put himself between us. Just in time, for Turner's sake. "The problem before us all is that we have work to do, and when I say we, I don't have a turd in my pocket."

"A what?" said Turner.

Frank ignored him and walked to a large street map of the city covering the far wall. There were pins with little numbers on paper flags stuck into the map. To the right, a table was pushed against another wall, clean except for an empty folder and four or five stray sheets of paper.

Frank studied the map. "Tell me about the old trick-or-treater first."

After a sullen pause, Turner shrugged, walked to the table, and sat on it, his feet dangling. He yawned and rubbed his face.

"Allow me to begin, as they say, at the beginning," he said. "We impounded the body along with all the others we discovered today, make that Saturday, as we must be well advanced into tomorrow by now, at two o'clock thi... Saturday afternoon."

Turner's voice trailed off. He scrunched up his face, moved his jaw around in a circle, and forced his eyes open, big eyes, even bigger than Frank's, though not as prominent. He's very tired, I thought. I'm very tired, I thought. Why shouldn't I be? Up early, the trip back from Honduras, only to turn around and fly out here. *At least I still know what day it is.* He's very tired. He's more tired than he should be. And so on, until my tired thinking was arrested by that deep, official voice of his.

"At first, I doubted he was connected," Turner was saying. "It looked like a common mugging, but the costume bothered me so I ran a check."

He paused. Frank turned away from the map to look at him. "And?"

"And nothing." Turner shrugged. "Nothing in any U.S. File. So I checked Interpol, and what do you know, his name is Avrim Ben Hazi, Mossad, retired. Under a cloud."

Frank's eyebrows raised in surprise. "What's he doing in Interpol's files?"

"That was the very question I asked."

"Whooooom did you ask?"

"That I cannot tell you."

"That's twice now. Is this a good source? The same source?

"Different source and an excellent one."

"Does your boss know about these private sources of yours?" Frank studied him with a skeptical squint.

"You have met my boss," said Turner. "He does not speak. He blithers. I cannot reveal my sources to him."

"Private networks are dangerous things. Your boss may be a blitherer and hard to live with, but your network will get you killed."

"My boss is not just hard to live with," Turner insisted. "He will get me killed. I have been unable to establish his bona fides as a blitherer."

"That is a very serious charge, my friend," said Frank, "I trust you do not make it lightly. And I wonder why you trust us."

"Twice correct," said Turner. "I do not make it lightly and I do not trust you. Still, I must work with you. Let us just say that Nelson Hunsecker is not consistently stupid. The malady comes out of remission only when it can do maximum damage, usually to my best agents. Someday, I shall catch Mr. Hunsecker being smart."

"That's your reason for the network? To trap one idiot? Will you invite me to your funeral?"

"I said, I do not believe he is a genuine idiot."

"Yeah? He seemed pretty bona fide to me." Frank turned back to the map. "So what did your network tell you about Avrim Ben Hazi?"

"He was in Interpol's files because he was a renegade agent of the Wrath of God."

"I thought that kind of information came only from the Mossad itself," I interrupted. "Is it verified?"

Turner glared at me.

"So," said Frank, "we have the following corpses gathered in the morgue on a Saturday evening: a pretty young woman, a two-bit whore, the top solo East Block specialist, an uncontrolled KGB agent, a renegade Israeli assassin, and four others who are...?"

"Two Americans, unknown, and two others, completely unknown," said Turner. "Maybe you should take a look at them. You may be able to identify one or two."

"Maybe, but I doubt I could beat your network," said Frank. "I will look later. It is already one o'clock and you're about to fall off that table, son. Give me the scenario now, from the beginning, so Dr. Watson and I can get our beauty rest."

"Who?" Turner shook himself from a near drowse, jumped off the table, and paced the room to keep himself awake while he told us what he knew.

"According to the pathologist," he began, "the earliest to die was one of the four you haven't seen. We found him at Midway Airport on the South Side, pin number one. The round that killed him matches the lethal one in Jared."

"That would be Mack," Frank said to me. Turner stopped pacing and stared at him. Frank waved him on.

"Next came your Ivan, Nickolai Kolnichkov," said Turner. "He died in an empty garage just outside the approaches to Rick's sovereign house, pin number two on the map. The time of death was approximately midnight last night. The cause was a nine-millimeter parabellum bullet to the head, not on your watch list."

Frank looked at me and shrugged.

Turner continued in his deep, fancy voice: "Ivan was severely beaten, reasons unknown, probably to provide information of some sort."

"He provided verification," said Frank.

"Pin number three," Turner continued, "marks an apartment on the near North side where three were found, each killed by one of the weapons already mentioned."

"No new weapons? No other weapons?" interrupted Frank.

Turner stopped, rubbed his chin, and gave a negative shake of his head. "Two were shot in the heart," he said, "the third in the head, execution style. The two unknown Americans and the other mystery man were in this group. Time of death is estimated at between two and four o'clock Saturday morning.

"Finally, the Israeli was found in an alley on the north side of the city, in full Hasidic dress, dead from loss of blood stemming from a knife wound to the carotid. He died at about breakfast time. Pin number four."

Frank swiveled around like a top to look at me, making sure I understood that this was Mack's.

"Next we come to the apartment on Edbrooke, number five on the map." The FBI man stopped pacing to sweep his arm through the air in the general direction of the map. The overhead fluorescent light seemed to bother him. He rubbed his eyes.

The official tone lowered slightly. Was this emotion? I watched Turner's face. It was grim and the eyes streamed with fatigue, but there was no sign of any change since we met an hour before. *Such a familiar face.*

"A few minutes before eleven twenty-five Saturday morning," he said. "Mrs. Jared, first name Cordelia, came home from the store with groceries for the evening meal. She discovered that her sister, Concordia Stewart, aged twenty, who lived with them, was, ah, entertaining a guest in her room. Mrs. Jared reacted angrily when her twelve-year-old daughter, Janey, told her Concordia's boyfriend was in the house.

"We have been able to ascertain that the reason this upset Mrs. Jared is because her husband was due at any moment and he always insisted that no other person be allowed in the house when he was there. This edict included repairmen.

"The boyfriend was a white American male, about five feet, ten inches tall, long blond hair worn to the shoulders, blue eyes, muscular build. He worked as a stock boy at the local Jewel supermarket and went by the name of Jerome Wajinsky. They called him Jerry."

Turner looked at us with swimmy eyes. He shook himself awake again. "Before Mrs. Jared could do anything about the guest, her husband, Eben Jared, burst through the apartment door. That is precisely the word she used, 'burst'. This door enters the living-slash-dining room. Concordia's room also opens to the living room, opposite diagonally to the front door."

Turner gestured ineffectively, trying to make us see the layout of the room he was describing. I nodded as if I understood, and he continued, "Jared shouted to his wife, who was standing to his left, and to his child, seated further left at the dining table doing her homework, 'Let's go now. We have to go now. Hurry up.'"

In Turner's low, official voice, Jared's words came over in equal, melodic pieces, scrubbed clean of the terror that had made the man shout.

Turner rubbed his temples and looked down at his feet. He took a deep breath, dropped his hands, and began to pace again.

"At that moment," he said, "the sister's bedroom door opened and several things occurred more or less simultaneously. A male voice in her room shouted 'No!' Jared drew and fired his weapon, killing the sister in the now open doorway. The boyfriend appeared partly in the right half of the doorway and fired at Jared, who was diving to his own right. A round hit Jared in the right arm and shoulder. His gun landed several feet behind him against the wall.

"At that moment, Mrs. Jared heard the front door close. She saw two men inside, both holding semi-auto handguns. One of these men bolted the door. There was a pause. The boyfriend, Jerry, now out of the sister's room, stood to Jared's right, the other two men to his left. The other two men were as follows: one was a blond man of about forty, with a mustache, wearing greasy blue jeans and a plaid flannel jacket. The other had long dark hair, greying and tied back in a ponytail, dark eyes, and a beard. Mrs. Jared and her daughter both recognized him as a Cajun from Louisiana who worked in a pizza parlor across the street. The little girl also knew him as the boyfriend of the woman across the hall.

"There ensued a brief discussion in what Mrs. Jared insists was Russian, between her husband and the older blond man. At some point in the argument, the younger man, Jerry, pointed his weapon at the little girl and prepared to fire. The Frenchman formed a sight picture on Jared's wife. Eben Jared then made a sudden move, reaching into his coat with his wounded right arm. The older blond man fired, killing

Jared instantly. The ballistics match number 1656Y on your watch list."

Frank nodded politely.

Turner continued rapidly with no trace of his earlier solemnity. "There was now a brief, heated discussion in German among the three assailants. It was, perhaps, a disagreement. The older man ordered the other two out of the apartment. They complied and he followed. This concludes my briefing. Are there any questions?"

"Did Jared have a backup?" asked Frank.

"No. There were no other weapons on his person."

"Thank you. You have told me volumes in a few short sentences. But you will have to spell out your little joke to Steve. He didn't notice it."

"What joke?" I asked.

"The conclusion of my briefing. Did not you recognize it?" said Turner.

"Did not you?"

"Sorry. I read a great deal of early nineteenth-century literature."

"In the Air Force?"

"Pardon me?"

I had a hard time seeing him; my eyes watered in the bright light. Was he swaying? "It was the standard Air Force briefing, " I said. "Were you in the Air Force, Mr. Turner?" *And during which century?*

"Please, call me Jay."

Frank interrupted. "I hate to break up this rapproch...
this reconcil... your making up like this, but we must be going now. Shall we say, until eight tomorrow, or rather this,
morning?"

"Yes, of course," said Jay. "Where?"

"Let's meet on Edbrooke, but let's not all drive right up
to the door. We can walk the approaches and meet across the
street, in front of the pizza place."

"Very good." Jay walked to the door, but before he
opened it, he turned back to Frank and said, "I must warn
you about one thing. I will be required to introduce you to
Cordelia Jared, and she may not cooperate with you because
of me. The interrogation this afternoon took several hours,
and she made it quite clear that she despised me at every
minute."

"Why was that, do you suppose?" I asked.

"I am a tool of the police state in her eyes."

"So you don't think her dislike has anything to do with
your unmistakable charm?"

"What is that supposed to mean?"

"Nothing. Nothing. Keep your sense of humor—if you
have one."

"I have one, MIG Fodder. I simply will not waste it on
such a poltroon."

Frank dragged me down the hallway.

"What's a poltroon?" I asked him.

"Let's go," he said. "We'll talk."

SIX

Frank fiddled with the heater. He started the engine of his rental car but did not put it in gear. The heater spewed cold air at us. Frank warmed his hands over it; they were that cold, that cold air could warm them, mottled pink, grey, and yellow, with little blue veins bulging from the backs.

"Let's go over what we know," he said.

"Why here?" I asked. "Wouldn't the secure room with the map be better?" *Read, warmer.*

"It's not secure."

"Jay seemed pretty competent." And the room was heated.

"He's very competent. Super competent. And the room is secure in the sense that nobody would be able to listen to us except Jay."

"Do you think he would?"

"I know he would."

"Why?"

"A man who sets up and runs a personal network is no longer obedient to orders. He's in the game for something else. This is what can happen when a smart man works for a stupid one."

I looked at the sheet of ice on the windshield making halos out of street lamps. The heater blew a degree warmer, but it didn't matter to me. I wasn't minding the cold. Hunger now.... Frank's teeth clicked until he forced his jaw shut.

I said, "I wonder how Handsome Hunsecker manages to get promoted, let alone stay alive."

Frank revved the engine. "How? Look at him! He looks like a movie star and talks like a diplomat. It doesn't matter that he's got shit for brains. Then there's Jay Turner, with a mind like a steel trap and an understanding that flows with the Colorado down the Grand Canyon. But he looks like Godzilla and he's a pure pain in the ass. He'll never be promoted. And he's smart enough to know that. He is dangerous."

"So you think Hunsecker's a bona fide incompetent?"

"Yes."

"What about Jello? Have you ever thought...?"

"What about Jello? You mean, has he turned?" Frank laughed for a long time. "Jello's got twenty-five years' worth of bona fides, Steve. In all the time I have known him, he's crept along the edge of disaster, with only luck as a guide. He is completely consistent: if he touches an operation, he screws it up."

"How did Turner know I was an Air Force pilot, Frank?"

"Good question. He seems to know you."

"He is familiar, but I can't place him. Does that mean I'm blown?"

"No. You're blown when Charlemagne knows about you. From then on you'll be under their scrutiny at every operational moment, and maybe some other times."

I have to admit I had a short case of the willies when I heard the words 'under their scrutiny' and remembered the Israeli killer and his extra smile.

"So what's going on, Frank? Who are all those dead people in there?"

"That, my friend, is a network of some kind. All these guys have their own networks, Steve. That one in there was Jared's. I've never seen a whole network go like that before. But then, I've never seen Charlemagne use a new weapon before. What did Turner say, a Glock? Remind me to ask him how he figured that out." He laid his head back against the seat, opened one button of his shapeless overcoat, and closed his eyes. "You tell me now, my beamish boy, everything we know about this case."

I began to repeat Jay's briefing. Frank opened his right eye and swiveled it at me, like a knowledgeable fish looking at a hook. He was not looking for facts, he wanted mental gymnastics. I was to do those flips and somersaults needed to solve a logic puzzle. If Mary, Jane, and Sue are married to John, Ted, and Bill, but not in that order, and Mary is married to the baker and Ted is not the policeman, who is married to whom, and what are their occupations? I hate those puzzles.

I made a minor leap. "Sobieski is missing."

"Right," said Frank. "Where is he? He uses a Makarov. There is no sign of the Makarov. And who is the Glock?"

"Maybe the Glock was the babysitter."

Frank swung his head slowly, like the clapper of a bell striking negatives at the top of each arc. "No. No. No. No," he said. "Babysitters do not kill, Steve. Get that through your scrappy skull right now. Babysitters do not fight. They do not engage in operations. They protect their governments by maintaining a respectful distance from the nasty little details. Get that, get that now. You will be Charlemagne's social secretary and no more. You book their hotels and safehouses. You arrange for Mack to have his favorite Mercedes or whatever else may be appropriate. You scrub the area before operations begin. You protect the populace. You clean up afterward. You arrange payment. That's it. Ipso facto exacto."

He took a deep breath after the exertion. "The Glock was not the babysitter. The Glock is new. And Sobieski is dead."

"Not retired?"

"No. These guys do not have that option. They hunt and are hunted till they die."

"What about the life expectancy of babysitters, Frank? Do they retire?"

"I'm still around."

"Maybe Sobieski sat this one out."

Frank shook his head.

"Maybe Sobieski bought himself a new nine-millimeter."

"Come on, Steve. We have a description of the Glock shooter. Jerry is too young, too blond, and has too many fingers."

"Jay could have missed that detail." I rested my forehead on the dash. "No. Jay doesn't miss anything," I said through a yawn.

I sat up and saw Frank smile for the second time that night. "You have a long way to go, my boy," he said, "but at least you have transport for the journey. Now let's find time for sleep before our dance card fills up in less than six hours. I'll think aloud; you stay awake and listen.

"My guess is that Sobieski is dead. Retirement is simply not an option for a specialist. It's a technical impossibility. They need to gather intelligence to guard against attack, and they need to keep working to gather intelligence. Sobieski is not retired.

"Is he elsewhere?" Frank asked himself rhetorically. "Possibly, but I doubt it. It is not Charlemagne's style to split forces. Many elements in this operation are alien to them, but I think if Sobieski were alive, he would have been here."

A thought jerked me awake. I interrupted. "Frank, could they have split up? Had a fight? Disagreed?"

He considered it for a minute, or maybe he was considering how he would answer me, how he would convey what he knew, the way I know, I just know, where the runway is.

Don't ask me to put it in words; only let me point to it until you see.

He opened his hand, palm flat at the top of the steering wheel, and he did point, at nothing at all, or at the dark and cold, or at the morgue. "They..." he began and trailed off. "This isn't in the file because I have no proof, but I think these guys go way back, grew up together maybe." He looked at me. "I think a break-up like that would mean treachery of enormous magnitude, enough to kill them all, not just one." He flared his fingers again and pointed at the foggy halo around a parking lot light.

I looked up and said, "I see."

Frank gripped the wheel again, then let go. He stepped on the gas again and fiddled with the heat. Sighing, he sank back into his seat and looking at the ceiling, said, "What else do we know?" His voice sounded much more tired. "We know that whoever commissioned this operation provided an incompetent babysitter or no babysitter at all. That leaves out the Brits, at least, and the French and the Thais. I know the men who handle the Charlemagne account for those countries, and they are all very capable. Nor would any of them allow an operation to go on without a babysitter, even if they were so bold as to commission it on US soil."

"Excuse me," I said. "How do you know there was no babysitter?"

"Or the babysitter was incompetent," Frank repeated. "I know because of the woman across the hall. A competent babysitter would have had her out of danger well before the operation began. She was not necessary by that time and should have been held somewhere else until the danger was past. She did not have to die."

"Then why did the Frenchman kill her?"

Frank shrugged. "I don't know. I suspect she irritated him or got in the way somehow. The operation began shortly before eleven the night before and did not finish until after eleven the next morning. After twelve hours, it would not take much to make the Frenchman pull the trigger. One of the little things you will learn to do is remove the innocents from the scene before it starts. Remove yourself, too."

"I'm not supposed to stay with them?"

"Hell no. You'll get yourself killed!"

"But...."

"No but. We've been over this. Respectful distance. Don't forget. You're such a scrapper, I know you love a good fight, BUT THAT'S NOT YOUR JOB."

"What about Jared's sister-in-law, the pretty girl?" I asked. "Shouldn't she have been out of there too?"

"Concordia? No. She was necessary. She was the new guy's ticket into the apartment."

"So she had to die?" I remembered the pretty face in the drawer and ached a little.

"I didn't say that. I don't know what happened. She may have moved when she shouldn't have."

"You don't think the new guy pushed her out in front of him?"

"And then shouted 'no' like a rookie?" said Frank. "No."

"He was a rookie then," I said. I could identify. "That's why he missed." *God, don't let me miss.*

"Missed!" Frank gave me the frog-eyed stare. "He didn't miss, my dear boy. How could you think that? Where is your brain?" He searched the car for it, bobbing his head around the seat like a pinball on a bumper.

"Okay, okay, I'm fucking thick. Tell me why he didn't miss."

"They wanted to talk to Jared. The only way to do that was to disarm him. The new guy fired around a left corner disarming an experienced specialist in the process of a left-hand dive for cover. Brilliant shot."

"Why do you say they wanted to talk to Jared?"

"Because they did talk to him."

"Oh. Is that why you do this job, Frank? Do you do it to save an occasional bystander's life?"

"What are you getting at?"

"You seemed sorry about the death of the whore."

"Yes, I am. It was unnecessary."

"Then she was important enough to try saving."

"She was alive and human," said Frank. "Two attributes I find very important. I rather prize them in myself. Now, what is the problem?"

"What good is saving a life like that? I mean, where, exactly, do you draw the line."

My boss, the frog, metamorphosed into a crocodile. Of course, this business is predatory, but this was my first glimpse of the reptile in him.

"We do not draw any lines, Steve. We may wrestle with 'guilty' and 'not guilty' as verifiable facts of the shadow world, and these words may be equivalent to 'dead' and 'not dead' when we're through, but we do not place preferences on any lives but our own."

He looked at me like I was lunch, so I tested the water. I always do. I can't resist, especially in the presence of a dangerous animal.

"So if her life was so meaningful," I said, "why not spend Charlemagne's next fee on her? And now that she's dead, there is a bum in my hotel parking lot who could use the money."

He glared at me so I kept going.

"I just don't know if I'd spend a whole lot of energy saving the life of somebody like that bum. He begs. He reeks of booze. I can't see myself worrying about him unless...."

"Unless he's like you? Unless he agrees with you and looks like you and dresses like you or one of yours? Think about it, Steve. You want to define a life worth living. Did you put any money in his box?"

"No."

"Why?"

"He'd only drink it."

"Are you his momma now, Steve? Like hell you are. First, you want to give him Charlemagne's fee, then you want to tell him how to spend it. The truth is you hate him and you know that's not a noble thing, so you make excuses to assuage your conscience. You don't know shit about who he is, but you know who you want him to be, no matter how shitty he may find it."

I grinned at the crocodile. "Here's the extent of my heavy thinking, Frank: If he's my friend, I help him. If he's my enemy, I fight him. If he's neither, I leave him alone and expect him to do the same. Why did you pick me for this job, Frank?"

The croc withdrew and the frog returned, heavy-lidded. "You're a natural, my boy," he said softly. He sighed and looked out the windscreen. The engine labored in idle and produced only cold air through the heater vents. A hundred yards away the morgue was busy. A disaster somewhere spawned a stream of red, yellow, and blue lights, trucks, police cars, and grieving survivors.

I broke in on Frank's thoughts. "I'm getting close, aren't I?"

He did not answer. I was, in fact, very close. Frank was the rarest of government bureaucrats: he felt responsible. He treasured life because he saw so much death. He did not wield Mack's knife, but he wielded Mack and to him, it was the same thing. Like the ancient headsman, he needed absolution. Even this early in the operation, the hooker's death was a personal reproach, a disaster in the realm of responsibility.

"There is still so much we don't know," he said wearily. "We don't know who this new guy is. We don't know how or when Sobieski died. He was very much alive when I saw him eight months ago. And we don't know what they wanted Jared to tell them. We have work to do."

"And when you say we...."

He cheered up a little. "Right. We'll use your car tomorrow. Check your back and stick to your legend. Once I park this car at my hotel tonight it will no longer be secure and I won't have time to trade it in. Yours should be all right for a little longer. I hope."

"How do you know yours is secure? Jay's pretty sharp."

"All the alarms I set were in place when we opened it. Turner's people did not get in."

"Why won't your alarms work tomorrow morning?" I wondered what signals he set to tell him if the car had been disturbed.

"Because by then, Stevie boy, Charlemagne will know what hotel I'm in, what car I'm driving, and what I'm having for breakfast."

"But as long as the alarms are in place, the car will be secure."

"Not from the Frenchman. You have a lot to learn. The Frenchman can get in anywhere."

"The alarms?"

"He knows all my alarms."

"He's that good?"

"Even better. He's incredible. He has a gadget for every occasion, a tool for every lock."

"But why would they even care? I mean, they're gone, aren't they? All in a day's work; let's mop up and that sort of thing, right? Body count complete. Time to go."

Frank interrupted: "Are they, Steve? Did they wave to you at the airport? Did you throw them a kiss from me?"

"All right, all right. It's late. I'm fucking tired. I'm not thinking. I assumed they were finished."

"If they were finished, if Jared was the final hit, why bother to talk to him? What did they want him to tell them?"

"So you think they are still here?"

"I know they are."

"Verify," I told my boss. "What's your source? There have been no more bodies since this afternoon. They're gone."

Frank swiveled his round, hairless head so that it reflected the parking lot light above us. He kept his voice low; it was almost a whisper. "It's instinct, Steve. That's all. I have known them for almost twenty years. Something is very, very wrong here, and Charlemagne will not leave until it is finished." He paused. "I don't know why it isn't finished. I just know it's not. They are here. I can feel it."

...

It was past three when I parked my rental car in the underground lot at the hotel and walked to the elevator. The bum
was there, asleep sitting up, snoring. The bottle lay empty at
his side. I dropped a dollar bill and watched it float into the
box.

"Thank ye kindly, suh!" It was a loud, exaggerated
Southern screech that sent a shiver through me as I stepped
into the elevator. I heard him laughing as the door closed.

On the sixth floor, I relaxed a little. Sleep was so close—
on just the other side of my door—that it fuddled me and I
could not get the fucking piece of plastic with the holes in it
to work in the lock. As I fought with it, the elevator behind
me opened. I was immediately awake, straining my eyes
sideways, turning slightly to see who walked the sixth-floor
hallway at three a.m. A man stepped off the elevator and
crossed the hall. I remembered Frank's intuition as I slipped
a hand in my coat to pat my Smith & Wesson. Did he pause?
Business suit. Maybe forty. Maybe blond. Hard to tell in the
dim light. Could be Mack. *But I'm not marked yet.* Frank had
reassured me. The man entered the room next door to Charlie's, on the other side. My key finally worked.

I don't usually mind hotels, except the times when I'm
kicked out of the house, but by six that morning, my room
was a torture chamber. For three hours, I didn't dream, I
nightmared. Stupid dreams woke me every few minutes and
then refused to be remembered. I became obsessed with the
locks on the doors, both the one to the hallway and the one

that connected to Charlie's room, and couldn't sleep without having my back to one of them so that I had to check six every gigasecond or else grow eyes in the back of my head.

After another vague terror trance at six o'clock, I gave up and got up. I went to the window and opened the curtains. Street lamps below showed a street already busy with people moving around, walking, riding, running, making deliveries of newspapers, milk, and express packages, relieving another shift at work, or going home after being relieved. There was traffic forming streams of paired light beams, two-directional, and dancing on wheels, as if the conductor were live, and not just a set of colored lights on a street corner pole. I saw three near accidents right below my window. I imagined two drivers flipping each other the bird and a lady, a pedestrian, crossing herself as the cars swerved around her. I felt better. I left the curtains open because I needed to stay connected to the outside.

While I showered and shaved, I tried to figure out why I was so uncomfortable. It was the man in the room next to Charlie, I decided. He bothered me.

I had a good breakfast in the hotel coffee shop. The waitress was friendly and gave me a free newspaper. I read the funnies. The bum was not in the parking lot. No doubt he had embarked upon an entirely new life made possible by my dollar bill. In another year, he would be one of those remarkable success stories—all thanks to me.

All my alarms were in place when I opened the car. Sally might forgive me if I made it home by Christmas. Life was good even with a low ceiling over the killer expressway that led me south. I wished I could enjoy it more, but that guy in the hallway bothered me. There was something, some connection, something important, that I had in the crosshairs, but could not get a lock on.

SEVEN

We stood on a street corner and looked at the apartment building where Eben Jared hid his family for a decade right under the noses of his enemies. It was an older three-story building of dark brown brick with a common front entrance on the ground floor. Rusted metal fire escapes hung on the sides, as ugly as barnacles but not as secure. An eight-foot wall ran behind this and all the other houses on the block. Behind the wall was an alley.

"He had a perfect view of two streets," said Frank. "It's not actually on Edbrooke, is it?"

It wasn't. It was at the top of the "T" where 105th Street crossed the end of Edbrooke. The building was offset so that the east-side apartments looked down both streets. The Jareds lived on the top floor, eastern side, front apartment.

"Tell me, Steve, where would you start if you wanted access to that apartment?"

We stood in front of the pizza parlor across the street, looking at the right, or eastern, corner of the building.

"I'd start by trying to get into the apartment behind it," I said.

"Why?"

"They share a fire escape. It looks like the kitchen windows are connected."

"Good. Where else?"

"Across the hall, of course; the western apartment."

"Of course. And where would you position yourself to watch?"

"Right here, " I pointed to the pizza parlor. "Or from one of these houses on this side of 105th Street, east and west of Edbrooke."

"Good. How would you do this without alerting Jared's watchers?"

"By blending with the neighborhood." I thought for a moment. "I'd move in slowly, one at a time, and establish my bona fides over several weeks or even months before the operation."

"Excellent," said Frank. "Make it months. Jared was very good. He would have noticed any flaws." He looked past me down the street. "Here comes Turner."

Jay was still two blocks away, walking toward us. I thought I would fill the time and impress my boss by telling him about the marks left by wedding rings. I had opened my mouth to speak when I glanced at his hand. No sign of a ring. I would sound like a rookie, which I was, or worse, like a fucking fool, which I like to think I'm not. My throat was already making a sound though, and I had attracted Frank's attention, so I said, "I sure could use a cup of coffee."

He stared at me for a minute before saying, "That's not what you were going to say."

"How do you know what I'm thinking?"

"Get used to it," he said. "Mack would have told you exactly what you were going to say and why you changed your mind. I only know it had something to do with hands."

"What about hands?" Jay asked as he walked up.

"Nothing. Good morning." Frank was abrupt. "Let's go. I want to see the apartment across the hall first, then if you will introduce us to the bereaved Mrs. Jared?"

"How should I introduce you?" asked the FBI man.

"With our names, sweetheart."

"Was that supposed to be a Bogie impression?" said Jay. "Frank Cardova and Steve Donovan of what, sweetheart?"

I must admit, Jay's Bogie was better.

"Of the government," said Frank.

"She will wish to know which government. She will want to see identification."

"Show her yours."

"She will want to see yours."

"We don't carry any. You'll have to vouch for us."

"She is not going to tell you anything."

"On the contrary, she will tell me much, no matter how little she says."

Turner took a key from his pocket and led us across the street and into the building.

Two pairs of doors faced each other across the third-floor landing. A small, dirty window provided light and gave a view of the street below.

"Convenient," Frank said when he caught his breath after the climb. "No back entrance. Where is the access to the alley?"

"Around the sides," said Jay. "Behind the building is a lean-to that covers concrete trash bins set into the alley wall. The shed is accessible from either side of the building. The bins open to the alley for garbage pick up. There are access doors through the wall every hundred yards, and a few holes."

"Any holes near here?" asked Frank.

"None."

"Doors?"

"At the front and on the West side of the building. Both secured with good locks."

"Perfect. First, let's see the apartment where the Frenchman's unfortunate lover lived."

Jay opened the door to apartment 3C. We were greeted first by a stench, then by a horde of surly cockroaches that scattered reluctantly from the cushions of a filthy sofa as we invaded their room. Plates and utensils still crusted with decayed food were stacked like a cockroach condominium on a sticky kitchen table at the end of the room. Torn and skimpy curtains tried and failed to lend modesty to a dirty window overlooking the street. The rest of the apartment was in the same state as the front room. The bathroom was a nightmare.

From Jay's explanation of the body's position and attitude, Frank concluded that the woman died, needlessly, for some minor interference.

"What I find hard to fathom," Frank said as he turned slowly in the muck, "is that Louis spent months making himself at home here. Who could pay him enough to eat at that table?" He looked at me, then at Jay.

"Run across the hall," he told Jay. "And arrange for us to meet the tenant in 3A."

"Which?"

"In 3A, the one that shares a fire escape with the Jareds."

"I already checked. She wasn't home and doesn't know a thing."

"Just do as I say," Frank said with some heat.

He stood in the front room of that filthy apartment staring at a cockroach on a wall. I cleared my throat, but he did not move.

"Frank," I said, "is it possible there was no commission?"

"What?" He broke his long stare and looked at me. "There has to be a commission."

"Why? Maybe there was no babysitter because there was no commission. Maybe this was something else. Have you ever known them to work without being paid?"

"Only if it is vital to their survival."

"If Sobieski is dead, maybe something happened that was vital to their survival."

"Maybe," admitted Frank, "but on this scale? There's an entire network in that morgue. Why? Why so many?"

"Could they be avenging Sobieski?"

"That is an emotional response."

"They are men."

"I have never witnessed an emotion in any of them, even the more volatile Frenchman, that was strong enough to sustain an operation for months in these conditions."

"If not money and not emotion, what then?" I asked. "Ideology?"

"No. You're right. It is not ideology. Their working philosophy runs pretty much along your lines: friends, enemies, and others. This has to be money or emotion. But if it is emotion, it's more than revenge for Sobieski or even their survival. And if it's more than that, my knowledge of them is next to useless. I have never known them to risk so much for so long. For any money."

"She'll see you now," said Jay formally.

Apartment 3A was barren and cold, but clean. There were a few cushions scattered on the empty floor and after Jay's introduction, Sarah Tisdale invited us to sit down. Our FBI guy declined the invitation and stood leaning against the wall near the door, hands in his pockets, with a bored, irritated look on his face. Frank and I sat down, cross-legged on the cushions. Frank folded himself carefully. It took a while.

"Thank you for agreeing to talk to us, Miss Tisdale," Frank said finally. He tugged on a pant leg that had twisted around his knee.

"Oh please, call me Sarah." She smiled at me.

Sarah was a young woman, pretty in a way, with long, blonde hair parted down the middle and worn straight. She wore blue jeans and a sweatshirt and reminded me of a girl I dated in high school. She reserved her smile for me. To Frank, she was respectful and distant. She ignored Jay except for an occasional malevolent glance.

"You're not cops, are you?" she asked.

"No," I said.

"But he is." She tossed her head in Jay's direction.

"Not exactly," said Frank.

"Well, he's got that cop look. I told him I wasn't even home yesterday. Do you want a cup of coffee or something?"

"No, thank you," said Frank. "Sarah, did you know the lady in 3C?"

"Who? Dottie? Not really. I thought she was kind of a pig, personally."

"You never associated with her socially then?"

"No."

"Or her boyfriend?"

Sarah looked puzzled. "Do you mean the guy from the pizza parlor?"

"Yes."

She took a moment to answer. "There was one time."

"One time? When was that?"

"About three months ago. September, maybe."

"Please, tell me about it."

"There isn't anything to tell. Dottie came over right after I moved in. She was real nice to me like she wanted something and asked me if I wanted to meet this guy her boyfriend knew. She said we should all go out together and have a good time."

"What did you say?"

"I said no. I wasn't sure our definitions of a good time matched. Then a couple days later, she came over again with her boyfriend, and he talked me into going out with his friend."

"What was he like? Dottie's boyfriend, I mean."

She hesitated a long time. "I liked him, and I wouldn't have minded him at all," she said frankly. "But Dottie was insanely jealous. I couldn't blame her. I don't know why he stayed with her. I don't think she knew why, either."

"And his friend? The guy you went out with, what was he like?"

"He was gorgeous!"

"Can you describe him?" asked Frank.

"He was just gorgeous. Blue eyes. Great body."

"Was he older, like Dottie's boyfriend?"

"No. He was like about my age."

"What color was his hair? How tall was he?"

"He was taller than you guys, but not too tall. He had an orange mohawk."

"A what?" I asked.

She smiled at me again. "You know, a mohawk. His head was shaved, like, on the sides." She ran her palms along the sides of her head, front to back. "And he had a huge mohawk spiked up in the middle, orange, like. He was gorgeous."

"With orange hair?" I wondered how I was getting all these smiles with a short brown haircut.

"Well, it wasn't him, was it?"

"I don't know, was it?" I knew I sounded a little irritated. Frank interrupted.

"Why do you say it wasn't him, Sarah?" he asked. "What do you mean?"

"There was this guy a couple of years ago."

"A couple of years!" I stopped at Frank's signal.

"Go on, Sarah," he said. "What about this guy?"

"Well, there was this guy. I went out with him once and he could really play the guitar. I couldn't believe it when he played, like, it was so beautiful. It made me cry sometimes. Anyway, he wore this black leather stuff with chains and spikes and all that and my dad had a fit. I couldn't get him to see that it was just because of the band the guy was in. He had to dress like that, but it wasn't him. He played the guitar and he wore that stuff so he could play the guitar."

"And the guy Dottie's boyfriend introduced you to?"

"Same thing. I thought maybe he was a musician. He liked music. We talked about it a little." Her voice trailed off as if she were tired of the subject.

"But you didn't hit it off?" said Frank.

"No."

Frank waited. When she didn't explain, he asked why.

"Neither one of us wanted to."

We waited again, for what seemed a long time. Sarah looked at Frank and explained. "He scared me. They both scared me. Something else was going on. It was like they were disagreeing about something without even talking about it. Dottie's boyfriend kept giving my date these looks, and...."

"And your date?"

"He was like, defiant, or something. Anyway, he didn't want anything to do with me. It was mutual, really."

We thanked her and unfolded ourselves from her cushions.

At the door, Frank asked her one more question: "Did you ever see him again? Your date, I mean."

"Yes." She said it steadily, as if she expected the question. "I saw him at Gately's. He was with the girl next door. I don't know her name. He bought her a tape. His hair was down, tied in back, and it wasn't orange anymore, but I'm sure it was him."

She gave me another smile before she closed the door.

"Time, gentlemen," said Frank in the hallway. He seemed to be in a better mood. "Time is the critical element here. And now it is time to impose our obnoxious presence on the family of the lately deceased. Lead the way, my beamish boy!" He pushed a reluctant Jay Turner none too gently toward the door of apartment 3B.

EIGHT

C hilly, frozen, sub-zero, outside on a December day, and inside apartment 3B. The flat was warmly decorated for Christmas, an orderly, comfortable home, but its mistress, the breathtaking Cordelia Jared, was neither warm nor genial. She frankly hated us and said so with perfect brown eyes. She was more a chiseled sculpture of an aristocrat than a real woman, with a long, graceful neck held stiffly defiant.

She singled out Frank as the major bad guy in her life, evicting Jay from that special loathsome place in her granite heart. Many things were said at first, none of them fruitful, not printable, either. We managed to seat ourselves, without invitation, around a dining table standing a few feet from the entrance. The living room stretched before us, with a decorated Christmas tree at the far end in front of the window. There were lights on it; I could see the wires dangling from the lowest branches, but the lights were not turned on. The carpet was light grey with damp, pink patches where the nap had been rubbed up, one near the tree, the other across from the entrance at the door of a bedroom. The kitchen was open to our left. I could see the fire escape past a little white valance with a lace fringe.

After a series of monosyllabic answers from the magnificent statue, Frank seemed to make a decision. "Listen, Ma'am," he said, leaning forward in his chair to throw the words at her. "We are enemies. Make no mistake. We are as opposed as ever two people can be. You are right. I do a nasty, secret job to stop your money backers from ever getting into a position to tell me what sort of shampoo I must use on my hairy head. Your husband did a nastier secret job for your benefactors' side, and if you didn't know that, I'm telling you now. For the first, and probably only, time in our diametrically opposed lives, we have a common purpose: to find out why your husband is dead. Now answer my questions, Ma'am, and if I discover any truth in this matter, we might strike a deal along the lines of I'll Show You Mine If You Show Me Yours."

He opened his coat and showed her his gun. "Your late husband and I were in the same secret business, different companies, same ID cards, and we had no trouble recognizing each other. The fact is, I am the only one on either side with the expertise to unravel this thing. Whether you get any answers when I do unravel it will depend on the answers you give me now."

He buttoned his coat and leaned forward again. "When did you know your husband would be home yesterday morning?"

"Friday." She was cold and reluctant, but cooperating.

"Who else knew?"

"Janey, my daughter, and Concordia, my sister."

"Did your husband know about Concordia's boyfriend Jerry?"

"Yes. Eben asked a lot of questions about him."

"Did he meet him?"

"No."

"What exactly did your husband want to know about him?"

"He wanted to know if he had an accent of any kind, and how old he was."

"He was satisfied with the answers?"

"Yes," she said bitterly.

A young girl came into the room. She was a copy of her mother, with skin perhaps a shade lighter. Her hair fell in soft brown clouds around her shoulders, and she moved with surprising grace despite the long, ungainly limbs that marked her preadolescence.

"You must be Janey. Please, sit down." Frank stood up and pulled out a chair for the child.

"No," said the mother. "She's been through enough."

"Sit down, Janey. We were discussing your father," said Frank. "Can you tell me what his job was?"

The girl glanced at her mother, received a tired nod, then looked at Frank. Her eyes were swollen and her voice had a nasal tone. "He was a salesman," she said. She looked again at her mother but could not catch her eye. "He did something secret," she said softly.

I caught the shock on Cordelia Jared's face before she masked it.

"How do you know?" asked Frank.

"I helped him sometimes," said Janey.

"That's enough. Leave her alone," said her mother.

"Tell me about your Aunt Concordia, Janey," said Frank, ignoring the mother.

"Concordia was a saint," Mrs. Jared interrupted. "She was sweet and trusting, never...." Tears intruded. She put her face in her hands to stop them.

"She sure was a saint," said Janey. "Jerry said so, too."

"What did Jerry say?" Frank asked gently.

"He said she was like his sister. So was I, he said. Except Concordia acted like her, and I looked like her. That's what he said. I asked him if his sister was black then, and he said no, but she was a princess just like me."

"He has a sister?" asked Frank.

"He had a sister," the girl said. "She's dead."

"Did he say when she died?"

"No."

"Did he say how she died?"

"No."

"Do you remember when Jerry and Concordia started going out together?"

"In October," said Janey's mother.

"When in October?"

"I don't know. About the middle of the month, I guess."

"Were they serious?"

"Very," said the widow. "At least Concordia was. She was in love. She thought he was, too."

I could almost taste the bitterness in her words.

We spent the next hour reconstructing the three-minute episode of the day before. Frank stood in each position as Janey and her mother remembered it. As Mack, he pointed his gun at an imaginary Jared; as Louis, he stood by the door.

"The Frenchman never moved from here?"

"He didn't stay there, but I did not see him move," said Mrs. Jared. "I was watching Jerry. He was going to shoot my baby."

"Try to remember where he moved to, Mrs. Jared."

She concentrated for a minute. "He was next to the table by the time Jerry put his gun away."

Frank stepped to the table and crawled under it. He pulled something from underneath, stood up, cracked a small square wafer-like object in two, and tossed the pieces to me.

"A souvenir," he said. "An insect of the genus spiesmus lissenus. Let's hope we can continue in privacy."

He turned to the girl. "Was Jerry going to shoot you, Janey?"

She swallowed before answering. "Yes."

"What stopped him?"

"The other man."

"Which one?"

"The blond one. The one who looked like him."

"Looked like him?" Frank seemed surprised.

"Yes," agreed Mrs. Jared. "They did resemble each other. I would say they were related."

"It was Jerry's dad," said the girl.

"Why do you say that?"

Janey squirmed and threw an embarrassed glance at her mother. "When Jerry tried to argue," she said, "he got that look that says don't argue. He stopped talking back and put his gun away."

"What look is that?"

"You know. That look. My mom knows how to do it, too." She did not look at her mother.

"Yes, Janey, I know," said Frank. "It was a parent look, wasn't it?"

She nodded.

"But the other man argued, too, the one whose gun was pointing at your mom?"

"Yes. But that was different."

"When Jerry put his gun away, was he angry?"

"No. He looked relieved."

"And the other man?"

"A little angry, maybe, but more..." she wrinkled her nose in an adorable expression as she searched for the word.

Mrs. Jared supplied it. "Puzzled," she said. "He didn't seem to understand."

"Did you understand anything that was said?"

"No. I think it was all in German," said Jared's widow.

"I remember a word, though," Janey volunteered. "All three of them said it when they argued."

"What was that?" asked Frank.

"It sounded like 'rocka.'"

"Rocka?" Frank thought for a minute. "Do you mean *Rache*?" He pronounced the German 'ch' from the back of his throat.

"Yes, that's it."

There was a pause in which no one spoke or moved.

"Mrs. Jared," Frank said finally, "to your knowledge, did your husband ever carry more than one gun?"

"No."

Another pause. We all stood as still as the Christmas tree by the window. Frank was looking at it. I watched Cordelia Jared. Her eyes strayed to the tree and began to fill again with tears. Frank broke the silence.

"I thank you for your cooperation," he said quietly. "We will go now. I cannot tell you much, but I give you this. Your husband died to save you and your daughter. By reaching for a gun he did not have, he forced them to kill him. Once he was dead, there was no longer any point in threatening you. Whatever else he was, he was a brave man, and he loved you."

"So what the hell does 'rocka' mean?" Jay asked in the hallway.

I answered, "Revenge."

NINE

"That's interesting," said Frank.

We stood in the front doorway of the apartment building, bundled against the cold with overcoats, scarves, and gloves in various shades of black or grey. Jay and I stamped our feet in a not very subtle attempt to get Frank to stop standing there and do something, or at least say something. It struck me that we resembled the three blind mice, and I suspected Mack was around the corner with a carving knife, waiting to cut off our tails—or worse. When Frank finally spoke, Jay and I frowned at each other.

"What's interesting?" I asked.

"That gas station, down the street," said Frank. "From the window upstairs, all you see is the canopy over the pumps, but from here, you can look right into the shop."

Jay looked at the station to our right. "I checked it out myself," he said. "Nobody's been there." He stamped his feet impatiently. "What do you want to do next?"

"I don't know. What do you want to do, Mr. Turner?" said Frank.

"I want to show you the other four bodies in the morgue and then take you to the apartment where we found three of them."

"What about you, Steve?" Frank asked me.

"I want lunch."

"Good plan. It's only eleven. Let's do the apartment first and save the morgue for after lunch. We'll take Turner's car."

It took us an hour to get to the apartment on the city's north side. It was on the top floor of a white brick building on a tree-lined street. The apartment itself was in perfect order and nothing seemed disturbed or missing. The only sign that three men had died there the day before was a small blood stain on the carpet, not rubbed pink, where one had been found with an execution-style bullet in his brain.

We walked through each room. All the fixtures, furniture, and even the kitchen utensils had a generic quality. It reminded me of a safehouse. There were two bedrooms furnished as bedrooms and a third, smaller room that had been turned into a darkroom.

"Any photos?" Frank asked Jay.

"None."

"None? No films?"

"Nope."

"Negatives?"

"No."

Frank looked at me. "I don't suppose there is a restaurant around here where we can have lunch?" he asked.

"I noticed a place around the corner," I said.

"Thought you might've."

At the restaurant, there were bread sticks in a jar on the table. I helped myself.

"Mrs. Jared is a beautiful woman," I said before starting on a second stick.

"And rich," said Jay.

"You mean all the money he must have left her in Swiss accounts?"

"No. I don't think she is aware of that yet. I mean that she comes from a wealthy family. Her father was a banker."

"A banker?"

"Yes. And I don't mean that he was a teller. He owned the bank. I grew up in Cabrini Green."

"What's that?"

"A housing project on the south side of the city. My mother cleaned windows for the city for twenty years to get me out."

"I sense some animosity toward Mrs. Jared."

"I had a scholarship to the University of Chicago," he said, "until she spoke to the scholarship committee. Irregularities with my essay, she said. Not the content. No, her concern was that I could not cite my sources. What sources? It was a personal essay, an original composition. No, it could not be, she said. No one writes or speaks that way."

"Speaks what way?"

"The way I speak. People think I am pompous, or that I put it on to impress, but it is natural to me. I grew up reading English literature. Most of the alternatives in my neighborhood were deadly."

"But you did get your degree?" I asked.

"Yes, of course. I attended an out of state university."

I swallowed quickly in order to make a sympathetic noise and gave myself the hiccups.

Frank said, "Try holding your breath, Steve."

The waitress brought our food. Jay and Frank dug in; I was too full of breadsticks.

"So this is personal, not political. Am I right?" I asked Jay. "More of an in-house, a family feud, not some political struggle? Between you and Cordelia, I mean."

Jay's frown was almost a relief after a brief smile. Ancient stone idols should not smile. The gods are invariably angry. I was used to life that way and had no use for a joker in the heavens.

"All politics is personal, Steve," he said. "It is a trade in personal power."

"You fixed-wing flyers are all the same," said Frank. "You think politics is an airplane with two static wings, left and right."

"Isn't it?" I said.

"No."

"Then what is it?"

He swallowed his last French fry. "It's a helicopter, Stevie, my boy. There's just one wing that's moving all the time, and when you look at it, you see shadows of where it's been and where it's going." He took a French fry off my plate and twirled it to illustrate. "You see, there is no left or right. There is only the center and the edge. If you sit on the center, you get dizzy." He rolled his eyeballs around; I could have sworn in different directions. "If you sit on the edge, you get flung off. And if you try sitting somewhere in between, it cuts you to pieces."

He ate my French fry.

"There's another rotor behind," said Jay. "Spinning perpendicular to the main one. It keeps the torque of the engine from destroying the aircraft."

Frank looked at him and pushed my plate toward him. "Have a French fry," he said.

"So where are you on the chopper?" I asked Frank.

"I'm on the edge, holding on."

"Jay?"

"Ditto."

"And WEDGE?"

Frank shrugged. "Maybe they're somewhere on that back rotor."

"Aren't they Nazis or something?"

Frank choked on a fry. "Good god, no. Where'd you get that idea?"

"You said they never work for the Soviets."

"I didn't say never. But that WEDGE is not one or the other, I can testify. We've had a commission or two against Nazis. WEDGE has always taken the paper, at great personal risk, I might add, since they top a few Nazi hit lists."

"Then WEDGE is not left or right?"

"Use the chopper, Steve. Maybe they're on that back rotor." He shrugged again. "I don't know. In the day-to-day mess of this business, everybody on the chopper bleeds red."

"And everybody," Jay tried to swallow a mouthful of my French fries. "Everybody is trying to get into the pilot's seat."

"Not everybody," said Frank. "Some of us are content to keep certain people out of it."

"Sometimes to keep them out, you have to occupy it yourself." Jay was not joking.

...

Eben Jared and company were in their assigned places at the morgue. Frank did not recognize any of the three that were found in the apartment, but when Jay opened the last drawer on the bottom right, he flushed red to the top of his hairless dome.

"You know him." The FBI man was not asking.

"Yes," admitted Frank.

"Who is he?"

"I'll tell you later. I need to think."

"I need to know now."

"No. You don't."

"If you want any further help from me...."

"Don't you threaten me, my friend. I will tell you who this is when I'm damn good and ready."

It was my turn to pull Frank shouting through the echoing hallway, out of the building, and into the grey day where I hoped the air would cool his temper. We waited for Jay in the parking lot. I wanted them both to calm down before I had to ride back with them to Edbrooke.

"So who was it?" I asked Frank.

He looked afraid. He later denied it, but he was afraid.

"So much for your no-commission theory," he said.

"Why? Who was it?"

"Anatoly Lupin."

"That tells me a lot. Who?"

"He was a babysitter. A high-ranking babysitter."

"Whose?"

"The Bulgarians'"

"Jared's?"

"No."

"Part of Jared's network, then?"

Frank shook his head. "With all due respect for a dead babysitter, Lupin was not somebody I would include in a private network. Jared certainly would not have."

"Bit of a Jello, was he?" I asked. "Why are you so sure it was a private network?"

"Everybody else is outside established control, and the connections are unlikely, especially the Mossad killer. Only personal connections can explain it."

"But Lupin?"

"He had to be assigned. Neither Jared nor Charlemagne would have consciously chosen to work with him."

"He could have been assigned to Jared."

"No. Jared had a very competent babysitter of his own."

"Are you telling me the Bulgarians commissioned Charlemagne?"

"No, the Soviets. Sometimes the Bulgarians act as their cutouts on wet operations."

"Disturbing," I said. "But I can handle it now that the world is a chopper. Why does it bother you so much?"

"It doesn't. I just don't like unexplained, unexpected developments, that's all, especially when one of them affects me—and you, I might add—personally."

"What's that?"

"Lupin was the first to die. It seems Mack has lost what little tolerance he once had for incompetent babysitters."

TEN

"**B**ut you're not incompetent!" *And I won't be incompetent.*

"You think so, do you?" Frank's breath made a fog around his chin.

For a minute I wondered what he was answering, my words or my thoughts. I said, "Yes, I think so."

"Define incompetent."

I thought about it. I thought about every bureaucrat I've ever been tempted to throttle. "People who are incompetent," I said cautiously, "take shortcuts or make long detours at the wrong places and don't even know they're lost."

"I think Mack's definition is anybody who makes a mistake," said Frank.

"But that's everybody."

"Right you are. I like your definition better, but you're not the guy with the knife."

"Speaking about the guy with the knife," Jay said as he stepped over a cement parking marker and rubbed the frost off an old car. He walked toward us. "It seems he met my boss last night. I just received word. I have been promoted. Do you think this investigation will take much longer? I have quite a lot to do."

Frank stared at him incredulously. "Are you saying Hunsecker is dead?"

"Yes."

"How?"

"It appears his throat was cut." Jay shrugged, as though such a thing could be in question. "They found him in an alley a few blocks from here, dead since about one o'clock this morning according to the pathologist. I had him impounded along with the others. Hunsecker, that is, not the pathologist."

Frank handed him a wadded-up piece of tissue from his pocket. "Here. Wipe the tears out of your eyes and get a hold of yourself."

We didn't say much on the way to Edbrooke. At first, I thought Frank was quiet because he considered Jay's car unsecure. But Jay couldn't even get him to make small talk.

So how come Frank, of all people, wouldn't talk? Was he still mad about their argument over the Bulgarian? No. The look on his round face was grim, not angry. Did he think Jay Turner killed Hunsecker? Impossible. Jay was with us until after two that morning. This new mood in Frank was a puzzle.

Something occurred to me. I dismissed it before it had a chance to fully form in my mind, but it intruded again, and I remembered a few details that seemed to support it.

One of the details I remembered was Jay and his mysterious sources. Frank said Jay was running his own network; he had stepped outside of control. I suddenly knew better, because I remembered where I had seen him before—at the Academy. Jay Turner was cadet Wing Commander during

my first, my doolie, year. He was a zoomie, and not just any
zoomie, but a successful, distinguished, disciplined graduate
who knew how to wend his way through the moral
labyrinth of any hierarchy, no matter how imperfect it might
be.

Jay Turner was under orders. The question was, whose
orders? As we drove south, only two minutes from our des-
tination, my thoughts followed each other like an elephant
walk, nose to tail, so closely that I had the answer before the
FBI man turned off the engine.

Jay was dedicated to two things: personal success and
ideological victory. He wanted to be in the pilot's seat for a
combination of reasons, like his mother and his scholarship.
Were there more? Hunsecker blocked the way. Chances were
also good that Jay was right about the man's allegiance. He
was not wrong about much. Cooperating with Charlemagne
was a perfect solution, from his point of view. They were
ideologically close (or so I thought); his cooperation would
not compromise his patriotism (or so he thought—he did not
yet know about the Bulgarian), and payment? Hunsecker.
Jay Turner was not interested in money.

"Do you know who the watchers are?" Frank did not
move his jaw much. It reminded me of Bogie again, but
Frank was not playing this time. I squirmed in the back seat.

"We know two of them," Jay answered.

"Any foreigners living on the block?"

"Yes. An old Czech woman next door to the pizza parlor."

"Convenient," said Frank. "You're sure she is not a watcher."

"Yes. At least not for Jared."

I bounced a little in my seat, trying to get Frank's attention. He ignored me.

"Did you find the Frenchman's apartment?" he asked Jay.

"Yes. It is next to the gas station. Jerry's flat is two blocks further down Edbrooke."

"All clean?"

"Very."

"No sign of the third man?"

"None."

"Would you introduce me to the Czech woman, please?"

Frank was at his most formal, chopping up his words into little pieces so they would fit through the spaces between his teeth.

"Certainly," Jay said politely. "Please lock the door as you get out."

I bored holes in the back of Frank's head with a laser stare, willing him to turn around.

We got out of the car and locked the doors in slow motion. Turner began walking across the street. I tugged at Frank's coat. He shrugged me off. A car came by and I yanked him back to the curb.

"We're being led," I whispered to him.

His eyes opened in mild surprise. "Very good".

"But it's a trap," I insisted.

"Most likely, but for whom?"

"For us. Let's get out."

"No. Never take your work home with you, I always say. You're not yet at risk. You can go."

"I'm staying."

"Then shall we see where we're being led?"

Jay stood on the front porch of a dilapidated little house with white lace curtains closed behind vertical burglar bars across the front window. There were two deadbolt locks on the door.

"Nobody's home," he said.

"Try again," said Frank.

There was no answer.

"Move." Frank stepped up to the door and pounded it with both fists and forearms six or seven times so that the door shook on its hinges.

We heard a timid voice from the other side. "Who is it?"

Frank pushed Jay forward.

"FBI," said Jay, holding his open wallet up to the spy hole in the door. "We would be pleased to ask you a few questions if you do not mind."

There were more locks than the two we could see. We heard each one slide aside in the full freezing minute it took for all of them to be drawn. When the door finally opened, no more than three inches, a small, wrinkled face peered at us wide-eyed with fear from a height of less than five feet.

"I have not done something wrong," she said with a thick East European accent.

"That's right," said Frank. "We just want to ask a question. May we come in?"

"Ask what?"

"It's cold out here. Please, let us in."

She stepped back reluctantly, her distrust and fear forming another, unseen doorway on the threshold. Frank crossed it boldly. Jay and I followed after a momentary hesitation.

"May we sit down?" Frank asked when the old woman did not offer us a seat.

She nodded. Jay and I sat on a worn sofa with lacy crocheted arm covers and a knitted afghan on the back. Frank sat in an armchair. A ceramic Christmas tree with tiny lights on each branch stood unlit on the window sill. On the wall next to the window, an old-fashioned pendulum clock tick-ticked in the silence.

"Won't you sit down?" said Frank, pointing to an empty rocking chair across from us.

The old woman sat down slowly on the edge of it, glancing at each of us furtively as if she were unsure which was most dangerous.

"Mrs?"

"Cgagny."

"Mrs. Cgagny," began Frank, "do you have a tenant in your upstairs apartment?"

She seemed alarmed at the question. "Yes," she said.

"Is he an American?"

"Yes. Of course." Too quick to not be a lie.

"And did you tell the watchers that?"

Her veined and spotted hands gripped the arms of her chair.

Frank prodded, "Was Czech his native language?"

"No."

"But he always spoke Czech?"

She froze again.

"Did he always speak Czech?" Frank insisted.

The woman shook. "Except once," she whispered.

"When?"

"When he first came. When he told me not to tell the watchers."

"What language did he use then?"

"German."

"And what did his use of German tell you, Mrs. Cgagny?"

There were tears in the old woman's eyes.

"I only want to know his nationality. I don't care what else you heard in his accent, just his nationality."

Her face registered almost instant relief.

"He was Austrian," she said.

"Blond? About forty?"

She nodded twice.

"We'd like to see the upstairs flat now, please."

She did not move immediately.

"He won't be back. You can relet the flat. Please show it to us."

Upstairs there was not much to see, except a good view of the Jared apartment across the street from the front room window.

"Did you make his meals?" Frank asked the woman while he stared out the window.

"Yes."

"And you did the cleaning?"

She nodded.

We walked through the other rooms. A chest of drawers in the bedroom was empty. Frank opened the closet. Two plaid flannel shirts hung there, and a pair of blue jeans, clean and pressed but stained with oil. He took one of the shirts off its hanger and showed me the label. It said 'Made in USA'.

"There you go," he said grinning. "Now you know what size shirt to get him for Christmas."

"You did his laundry, too?" he asked the old woman.

"Yes."

"It's in character, anyway," he muttered. "You can give these away or use them as rags," he said to the woman as he handed her the shirt. "Like I said, he won't be back."

...

"What was she afraid of?" I asked when we were back outside. "Mack?"

"Somewhat, of course," said Frank. "It's the ordinary reaction to being in the same room with him. There are many fears in this world, Steve. I don't know which is her particular fear, but you can bet Mack knows, and he used it to keep her quiet."

He shrugged his shoulders and slapped his sides. "That was a nice waste of time, confirming what I already knew, wasn't it?" He looked at Jay. "Where next?"

Jay shrugged.

"Okay. I'll pick." Frank pivoted his round body on one toe and turned in a slow circle. "I pick... the gas station." He pointed down the block and smiled at Jay.

We began walking. Frank allowed the agent to get well ahead of us and said in a low voice, "Does Turner know what car you're driving?"

"No. I don't think so."

"Good. Keep it that way. We'll talk later."

Jay waited for us. We caught up to him saying nothing. We slowed again as he walked on.

"I forgot to ask her if Mack ever left for any length of time," Frank said when Turner was a safe distance ahead.

"Should we go back?"

"No time. The game's afoot, my dear Watson, and perhaps we will make up the mistake in the next interview."

"No doubt," I said. "It's not that important anyway, is it?"

Jay stopped and we repeated our speed up, slow down maneuver.

"It could be," said Frank when Jay went on ahead again. "The information could confirm if this operation is commissioned or private. As a point of instruction, I might add that Mack would not waste this opportunity to tell me what he thought of my mistake."

"Pleasant to work with, is he?"

"He is abrasive and insulting."

I stopped when Jay did. I had more to ask and we were only a few yards from the gas station. I tugged at Frank's sleeve.

"Why are we being led?"

He shrugged.

"If they're still here, if there is something else," I said, my mind spinning, "then there is another target."

"Indub... undoubt... certainly."

"So what are they waiting for?"

"Who knows? Timing? Verification? Any number of things."

"And what part are we playing in this?"

Frank looked at me steadily for a moment, then walked away without answering.

ELEVEN

George Douglas owned and operated the rundown service station on the corner one block west of Edbrooke. He was an older man, a little rundown like his business. But what hit me right away was that he looked just like Frank, only with dark skin and a magnificent mustache, maybe to make up for the lack of hair on his head.

Jay watched Frank and George curiously as they shook hands. He grinned at me. "The sun was shining on the sea," he said.

I didn't get it.

He rolled his eyes to the ceiling, frustrated with me.

"Excuse me, gentlemen," he said, sending me the eyeball signal You'd Better Get It This Time. "The time has come, the Walrus said…"

I got it. "…to talk of many things."

Frank and George stared at us. There were no mirrors handy to tell them they looked like each other and reminded us of Tweedledum and Tweedledee.

"Right," said Frank. "Mr. Douglas, do you mind if I ask you a few questions?"

"Go right ahead. Call me George. Can I call you Frank? That was your name, wasn't it? Frank?"

"Cardova."

"Right. Samantha!"

A tiny woman entered from the shop floor to the left of us. In a forest, I would have thought she was a wood sprite —light, compact, and mahogany brown. I found it impossible to guess her age, though she was not young. She exchanged many words with her husband that were largely unnecessary but which fascinated me, because of the way she spoke them. Her elfin face animated every word, bringing it to life. She shooed us into a room the size of a closet near the cash register and told us to keep the door open so we could breathe and she could listen in.

The room was a box, ten by ten, filled with a huge old grey metal desk. George squeezed into a chair behind it. Frank took the only seat in front. I wound up stuffed in a corner behind Frank, trying to face the door. Jay had the door position, making Frank and me uncomfortable, but we had no room to maneuver.

"Look at this mess," said George pointing to a pile of coffee-stained receipts and orders. "I don't know what I'm going to do now."

"Can you tell me," said Frank with undisguised impatience, "if you've noticed any foreigners in the neighborhood?"

George laughed. "You want to know about Mack?" he asked. "Go on. Ask. What do you want to know?"

A lot of significant glances bounced around that little room.

"When did he come here?" asked Frank.

"In August. He started in August."

"What did he tell you?"

"He said he was an illegal immigrant, but he was a good mechanic, and if I gave him a job, he'd make me a lot of money."

"What did you say?"

"I said I couldn't afford no trouble. He said he couldn't either, and that if trouble came close, he'd leave and I'd be in the clear."

"And you gave him the job?"

"Yep."

"And?"

"And he was a great mechanic. More than that. He didn't deal too much with customers, but he organized all the paperwork around here, did the ordering, and paid the bills. Like I said, I don't know what I'm going to do now."

"Do you mean he's gone?"

"Yes."

"You said his name was Mack?" said Frank.

"He said I should call him that," said George. "He said I reminded him of somebody who called him Mack, so that name would do."

Jay and I looked at each other.

"Can you describe him?" asked Frank.

"He was medium, I'd say, blond, mustache—not as good as mine, though. I gave him some grief for that. Got him to smile once in a while."

Samantha leaned through the doorway. "He was very handsome," she said. "I have half a dozen friends at church who would have gone out with him. Did you tell them how he learned to fix cars, George?" She supplied the answer without waiting for her husband. "His father's foreman taught him how to fix farm machinery when he was a kid."

She kept going. "I kept trying to fix him up with Roberta. She's a lovely woman. Blonde like he is, but I don't think hers is real. It suits her though. Anyway, he didn't seem interested so I decided on Chrissy Jones, but I didn't have any luck there, either. I was about to suggest a lovely woman in the choir—the traditional choir, not the Gospel choir. She's a soprano. Her name's Nancy. I didn't get a chance, though, because that was when he went away and before he came back, Nancy said she was moving, so I didn't see any point in fixing them up. Tell them about when he went away, George. They'll want to know that."

George was able to tell us because a car drove up to the pumps and Samantha went outside.

"One day," George began, "Mack was in his usual spot. He always pulled the cars in a certain way and had his tools laid out just so. He was working on a car that day, and I was sitting on a stack of tires trying to get him into some kind of conversation—not easy, mind you. This car drives up, nothing special, but newish, and out jumps this young man with the strangest haircut you ever saw."

"What was that?" asked Frank.

"It was short on the sides and long on top, and the long part was parted in the middle, combed down, and pulled back in a ponytail. Nice looking young man, though. Reminded me of Mack."

"What happened?"

"Mack dropped the wrench he had and looked like he'd seen a ghost. The kid comes up to him, and they couldn't have said more than three words to each other, but I don't know what they were. They weren't English. Mack wiped his hands on a rag and told me he had to leave right then, but he'd be back in a few days. I was worried there might be trouble or something, but he said not to worry, the trouble was all his and he would be back. I had a hell of a time with all the job orders he left behind, but he was back in three days."

Frank looked steadily at Jay for a minute, then back at George. "When was this?" he asked.

"October. In the beginning of October some time. I remember because it was the second Sunday in October when we finally got him to come over for dinner, and...."

"And we got him to come over because of my foolishness," interrupted Samantha, once again in the doorway. "When he came back, I was desperate to get him to go out with somebody. I was really afraid for him. He was so silent and withdrawn. Before then, he would watch everything going on. You wouldn't believe how sharp he was, but after that time he went away and came back, he did a lot of staring. His work was slower."

"It was," her husband agreed.

"After a week with no more than five syllables out of him, I was gonna make a match for him, and I didn't care who with, so I came right out and asked him if he preferred men. I didn't know any like that, I said, but you never know when one might turn up."

I thought at first that Frank was crying. He had his face in his hands and his shoulders were shaking. "Good Lord," he said, gaining control of himself, "I wish I could have seen his face."

George chuckled. "Sam can put her foot in it sometimes."

There was an uncharacteristic pause from her before Samantha launched again, this time in a lower voice. "He put down his tools and looked at me and said with that heavy, 'Cherman' accent of his. It was really heavy, but he understood everything, well, except once. He said 'Look Zamantha, I know you mean well, but I had a wife and recently lost her. Please do not suggest anything else.' I felt so bad. How could I have been so stupid?"

"I don't know," said George. "How?"

"Oh, stop it, George Douglas." She turned to Frank. "I wanted to crawl under a rock, but I managed to tell him that if that was the case, then he needed people while he was grieving and he better come to dinner that Sunday for his own good. He said he didn't like being around a lot of people, and I told him it would be just us. 'Please, please, come to dinner; I'm so embarrassed,' I said."

"He came?" asked Frank.

"Yes," said George. "He came and we had—an interesting time."

"I can imagine."

"We watched a football game and we talked a little. He talked a little. Sam talked a lot."

"You did your share," said Samantha.

"What did you talk about?" asked Frank.

"Our kids, mostly," George replied. "I asked him if the young man who came for him that day was his son. He said yes. We started talking about what we wanted for our kids. I told him how I managed to get three out of five of mine to college and the other two in good jobs. He said he'd been able to get his son to go to a university, but events were working against what he wanted for him. I didn't quite understand what he meant, but I got the impression there was a disagreement going on or his son was doing something he didn't like."

Samantha started to talk again, and I tried to understand how this tiny acorn of a woman could have produced five children, now grown. She was interrupted by Frank.

"Excuse me, but did he say how his wife died or when?"

"No. I didn't ask," said Samantha. "I figured if he wanted me to know, he'd tell me. I did ask him if he had any other kids."

"What did he say?"

"No. But he kind of choked on it. He was a lot more relaxed at dinner after he'd had a beer or two. But his table manners were dreadful."

Frank leaned over in his chair, looking for an explanation.

"He kept his knife in his left hand the whole time," said Samantha, appalled. "We had a pot roast, carrots, and potatoes, and he pushed everything onto the back side of his fork with the knife, then put it in his mouth upside down. I couldn't believe it. I told him that when he judged he was ready to meet one of my friends, I'd be happy to introduce him, but he'd be better off not taking her out to dinner until I could have a chance to show him some table manners. All five of my children have good manners."

I knew this time that Frank was not crying. He covered his mouth to muffle a guffaw.

"What did he say?" he asked through his fingers.

"He didn't say anything. He just stared at me like he was bewildered. It was the only time he couldn't understand plain English. I was going to explain it again, but George gave me the 'shut up' signal and I never got another chance."

"Was that the only time Mack came to dinner?"

"Yes. I invited him again a couple weeks later, but he said he was busy. I was getting ready to invite him for Thanksgiving, but then it happened, and... well...." Samantha ran out of words. She looked to her husband for help.

"It happened? What happened?" asked Frank.

"Things changed," said George.

TWELVE

George sat forward in his chair, put both hands in front of him, gnarled fingers flat against the beaten grey surface of the desk, and looked steadily at Frank.

"Back in September," he said, "we started getting robbed. It happened about every week or ten days. About the third time, Mack was at the register; I was in here, watching through that door. This guy comes in with a pistol, points it at Mack, and tells him to cough up the money in the register."

George's pause at this point seemed significant. Frank asked him what happened next.

"Mack laughed," said George. "The guy with the gun started gettin' mad and I told Mack to give him the money. He did, and the robber ran out, and Mack went back to work. He worked on that car that night until we closed at midnight. I heard him chuckle every so often. I thought it was a little strange."

We waited for George to continue. He drummed his fingers on the desktop in a rat-tat rhythm, as if deciding how to tell the rest.

"I kept getting robbed," he said, "but I got smart and stopped keeping more than a few bucks in cash on hand. Mack didn't usually work nights, so he wasn't here when it happened until about a week before Thanksgiving. That night, he was working later than usual, and six or seven of these guys come in. They're a pack of big, mean thugs, like them hyenas that steal and scavenge a lion's kill and act tough like it's their own. They want my money—as usual. I give 'em twenty bucks. They said it's not good enough. I better come up with more the next day, or I'm gonna get hurt. If I call the cops, they said, they'll burn the place down. They want a thousand bucks—for fire insurance.

"Mack heard the whole thing from the shop floor. I asked him what he thought I oughta do. I was kind of hoping he'd stand with me, but then, I was between a rock and a hard place. I needed Mack to help me and I needed the police, too, but the two were sort of mutually exclusive if you know what I mean."

We all nodded.

"Mack said I should give them the money. I said no way. He told me to be patient, give them the money now and things might get better later. There was no way I'd ever give that scum my money, I told him. He said he'd give me the money to give them. I said there was no way I'd give them any money whatsoever. I would fight them, I said, by myself if I had to. I was talking like a fool, but I was so mad it made me brave.

"The next night, Mack stays late. Everything is pretty quiet. I got a baseball bat in the corner, ready. The guy who works at the pizza parlor drives up and starts pumping his gas. The young man who came to get Mack back in October comes in and asks for change to use the candy machine. I see the gang that's trying to muscle me start crossing the street toward the station and I pick up the baseball bat from the corner. Mack tells me to put it down and go to the office and stay there. I say I'm staying. He says stay out of the way and let him handle it.

"So the gang comes in. One's got a big chain; two got pipes; another one carries this hammer. There's seven of them. I counted them later when they were on the floor. The guy from the pizza parlor comes in behind them, throws the bolt on the door, and pulls the shade. Then all hell breaks loose."

George looked at Frank steadily. "I've seen some fights, but I've never seen anybody fight like that. In about a minute, all seven are on the floor, groaning, bleeding, or both. Mack picks up the guy who was sorta their spokesman and throws him against the wall. He holds him there with one hand and the other hand's holding a knife against the side of his neck. I gotta tell you about this knife. I don't know where he got it from, and when it was over, I don't know where it went to. But from then on, I always knew he had it and it separated us some more."

George leaned back in his chair again and sighed.

"It wasn't all that big a knife, but you could see it was sharp, of course. Why wouldn't it be? It was the way Mack held it there like he was used to it. He was... comfortable. 'Course, the guy against the wall weren't comfortable.

"Everything gets real quiet except for a groan or two from the floor. Mack's son, the young one I saw in October, says in a low voice, 'You're out of your league, guys. We'll let you walk out of here now, but if you come back, you won't walk again.'

"The guy from the pizza parlor takes all the weapons these kids are carrying, breaks the blades on half a dozen knives, and does something to two guns. Then Mack, and the kid, and him, all set the bums on their feet and shove them out the door. The gang scatters. Some run, others limp. I ain't seen any of them since."

"Was anything else said?" Frank asked after a long pause.

"No. Mack's boy bought a candy bar and left. The pizza man paid for his gas. Mack took the money and put it in the till. Nobody said a word."

"What did you do then?"

"Nothing. I said thanks and left it at that. Mack went back to work."

"Mack's son," said Frank, "his English was perfect? No accent?"

"No accent."

"You said there was a change after this. Did Mack change?"

"No," said George. "I did. After that, every time I looked at Mack, I saw his knife. When I looked in his eyes, I saw somebody who could use that knife. He was no cowardly punk. He was a professional. I ain't no fool. And I figured he was here for professional reasons that I was better off staying out of. I stopped trying to draw him out about things. We didn't have anymore what you'd call conversations, just comments about work, the weather, that sort of thing."

"You seem disappointed."

"We were... well, I thought we were becoming friends," said George. He put his hands on the desk again and stared at them. "Sort of." He spoke mostly to himself, then looked up at Frank. "After that night, I knew that would never be possible, but then I suppose you gotta take it like it comes. We're acquainted. I don't know who or what he is or how much was a lie. We're acquainted; that's all."

"You haven't seen him since...?"

"Friday." George lifted his hands, slapped his palms on the desk, and stood up in one dismissive motion. He looked at Jay. "You look tired young man. Why don't you go home? I'll walk you to the door."

Jay scowled, and looked around, confused. Frank stood to go but was waved back into his seat by his twin. "Stay another minute," said George, "and we'll have a cup of coffee. Is this your man?" he asked, pointing at me.

"Yes," said Frank.

"He can stay, too." He took Jay's arm and pulled him through the door, saying, "You look too tired to go on."

"Wait a minute." Jay shook him off and looked at Frank. "What about tomorrow?"

"Same as today, I suppose," Frank said with a shrug. It occurred to me that he was not expecting a tomorrow.

Jay held out his hand to Frank, who ignored it. "Just in case," said Jay, "it has been a pleasure to work with you."

Frank stared ahead in silence.

"It will work out," Jay insisted, dropping his hand. "I will see you tomorrow." Was he trying to convince himself?

Frank said nothing.

George pushed the FBI man out of the little room none too gently.

"I'm not very good at this," he said when he returned to his seat behind the desk. "Sam!"

"What?"

"Coffee!"

"Don't you start that!"

"Please!"

"That's better." She stood in the doorway. She had three cups of black coffee with her.

"What do you have to tell me?" asked Frank, still staring ahead, not seeing the cup in front of him on the desk.

"I'm a live drop, you know," said George. "He told me that. He said to get rid of the FBI man and give you a message. This stuff is all new to me, but Mack said I wouldn't get nobody hurt. We had one more conversation before he left on Friday night."

"Tell me."

"I told him about my boy."

Frank's brow wrinkled.

"Mack was tense. Real still," George explained. "That was one of the peculiar things about him, the way he could be still, even when he was walking. He told me he was leaving. I asked if it was because of something going on with his son. He said no. But he was even more tense when he said that, so I jumped in the way Sam would."

"Thank you very much, George," said Samantha from behind the register.

George ignored her and continued. "I remembered how that young man fought those hoods in my shop one night, and I said, 'Is your boy turning out just like his old man?' I'll never forget the look on his face. I didn't need an answer and he didn't give me one. So I told him about my oldest son. I had so many plans for that kid. He was gonna be an astronaut. The first black president. He'd play for the Bears."

George took a sip of his coffee and cradled it in both hands. Samantha appeared in the doorway, silent.

"We did okay in fits and starts until he was fifteen," George continued. "Then I lost my job. Again. And we had nothing left. Sam and I weren't getting along and we had five kids to feed. I decided to leave. I was packing. My son came in and I saw his future. I could see him repeating every struggle I ever had, every stupid mistake, every misery. When he was born, it was like this new life had so many possibilities. He could do anything, be anything. But when I was packing that bag, I saw him surrounded by the same old shit. The poverty was the same; the fights were the same. Same. Same. Same.

"I put a shirt in the suitcase and remembered watching my dad do the same thing. All the changes I planned. I couldn't change nothing—nothing. I was sick of it. I was disgusted and trapped and so was my kid. I tried to say goodbye. He was sitting on the bed next to the suitcase, looking at me, and I thought how stupid I was for thinking he could ever play for the Bears. He was little like his mother, for chrissake. The same things that made me were making him and there was nothing I could do about it."

He took a slow sip from his cup. "Except stay," he said quietly. "I could stay. No, I thought. Impossible. And it won't do no good. All the other problems will still be here. He'll be shaped by them with or without me. I could only change one thing. I could stay. So I unpacked.

"Mack didn't say anything when I told him all this. 'I know it's not the same with you and your son,' I said. 'I don't know what your circumstances are, or his, and I suspect they're a lot different from mine, but the point is that if you can change just one detail in his history, do it. My boy's not an astronaut; he's not the president, and he's still too puny to play football, but he didn't go to jail when he was twenty like I did. He's working; he's happy, and he's got three fine sons. And I know his youngest will be president. The kid's a politician."

George looked at Samantha standing in the doorway and back again at Frank. "We know some people died yesterday in that building down the block that Mack was always watching. Sam and I are asking you to tell us one thing before we give you his message."

"Go ahead," said Frank. "I'll do my best."

"Did Mack's son kill somebody there?"

"No."

Both sighed and Sam bowed her head.

"But Mack did," said George.

"Yes."

Samantha moved first after the long silence and picked up the empty coffee cups from the desk.

"What did Mack tell you to tell me?" asked Frank.

"He said not to say anything to anybody except a man named Frank Cardova," said George. "I could make sure it was you, he said, by checking your gun. I said I don't know nothing about guns, so he told me to ask you what kind of gun you carry."

Frank opened his coat and showed his gun in its holster. "It's a Walther PPK."

Did I detect a hint of pride in Frank's voice?

"Yep. That's the one," said George. "Mack said, 'Frank looks like Elmer Fudd, but he thinks he is James Bond.'"

"I do not think I'm James Bond," said Frank tautly.

"Don't look at me."

"I wonder how he knows about Elmer Fudd?" I said.

"I asked him if Bugs Bunny was big where he comes from. He said he didn't know; he just had a lot of American cartoon tapes at home."

I tried to imagine Mack watching Bugs Bunny.

"Let's get to the message, George," Frank said wearily.

"You have an appointment with some guy named Slavin tonight at nine-thirty at Rick's."

I stood abruptly straight in the corner where I had been slouched against the wall. Slavin. Number three, Executive Action Department, First Chief Directorate, KGB. More than that, Slavin stayed in Moscow. He was an inner circle spook, with real information. They didn't let his kind out very often.

THIRTEEN

I checked my back as I walked to my car. Frank said he would meet me there in ten minutes. After fifteen minutes it began to snow and I began to worry. After seventeen minutes, I became aware of a black Mercedes parked on the other side of the street fifty yards behind me. Mack's favorite car, I remembered. I watched it in the mirror, through the back window. It didn't move; I didn't move. My back window was a painting, with a car as center subject; a car watching my car, I thought; I didn't know. I suspected.

My senses were trained entirely on that Mercedes so that when the passenger door of my car opened suddenly, my elbow came down on the horn, sending a long blast of noise down the quiet street.

"Lovely," said Frank climbing in. "You might consider locking your doors and paying attention. Just a suggestion."

"I was looking at that Mercedes."

"Yes, I saw it."

"Is it them?"

"No. It belongs to the people in the house where it's parked."

I looked at the house, a battered two-story, like the others on the block, with a boarded-up window and dead weeds poking through the snow. There were houses in better condition, but this was not the worst. The cars parked on the street and in a few driveways were similar to the houses. The Mercedes did not belong. I stared at Frank in alarm.

"The question, Stevie," said Frank, "is not whether, but when. When did it arrive?"

"I don't know."

"You didn't see it arrive? It didn't drive past you?" He shivered. "Turn on the heat, please. I'm freezing."

"I didn't notice it until about fifteen minutes after I got here."

"Did you check this car? You did have it locked, didn't you?"

"Yes. I unlocked the door for you."

"Don't do that again. Wait until I get here. Did you notice the Mercedes while you were checking?"

"No."

"So it drove up from behind you after you arrived."

"Probably."

"It's important, Steve. If it was here waiting for you, that means this car is already blown. If it came later, they simply followed you here and we can get one more use out of it before they touch it."

I thought for a moment, picturing the street as it was when I first unlocked the car. "It came later," I said.

"Let's go somewhere," said Frank.

"Where?"

"I don't care. Stick to busy streets. I want to see movement, traffic, activity. Where's the deck?"

"The what?"

"The tape deck. You said there was a tape deck in this car."

"There." I pointed in front of him.

He pulled a cassette from his coat pocket. "I need to think before we talk. Just drive and be quiet."

The snow became heavier, darkening the dusk and making unlit buildings into silhouettes of black on dark grey. Occasional yellow lights haloed a few windows and added a brown tone to the buildings. I turned on the headlights and wipers and watched the mirror as I pulled away from the curb.

"Well?" said Frank. "Have we grown a tail?"

"Yep."

"Turn left up here." He pushed the rewind button on the tape deck.

I turned left. The headlights behind me turned left.

"Turn left again on State Street, right at the next light, and keep going. Do you like Rachmaninov?"

"Who?"

"Never mind. Do you like music?"

"Of course."

"Who is your favorite composer?"

I thought maybe Frank wanted light conversation, a relief from the pressure that pursued us with the Mercedes.

"I like Dire Straits' new album," I said, "but my favorite is U2."

"Me too? Sweet of you Stevie."

"No. U2. The group, U2."

"That's an airplane. Must be why you like it."

"It's a rock group."

"I know. I'm trying to be funny. Not an easy thing to do right now. What was that other group you mentioned?"

"Dire Straits."

"Appropriate. Do you have any of that with you?"

"No. I didn't bring anything like that."

"Sometimes I need music; it tells me a story. Other times it helps me think. Okay if we listen to Rachmaninov's second piano concerto?"

"Sure." I had never heard of it.

"Is the tail still back there?"

"I can't tell anymore with all this traffic."

"Funny. I haven't even noticed the traffic." He pushed play.

I did not hear a story, nor did Frank's music help me think. It did what all classical music does to me; it threatened to knock me out, especially after a sleepless night and a full day. I fought to stay awake and on the road.

*Maybe Frank hears a story, but I'm hearing just bare chords on a piano.*I forced my eyes open

The chords gave way to a dark symphonic melody that rolled along strongly while the piano became more complicated behind it. The melody lightened, became less sad, and receded, allowing the piano to develop its melody, clear, different, but related. There was a light period when I thought I could not fight sleep, but new notes and chords began to sound a doom that shook me into a kind of half alertness. My eyes stayed open but my mind rested on the sound of that piano. It flowed like a light stream, going underground while something else developed. The stream surfaced again and quickened. Spurred into a rush by the crescendo around it, the piano became a torrent threatening its banks. It broke. The original melody began again, only stronger and yet overshadowed by the piano, no longer simple, nor light, but pounding an insistent melody of its own. A melody that complemented, was related to, was a logical outcome of the original, but was nonetheless different, new, a bit raw and discordant, but a necessary and inevitable addition.

"There he is," said Frank, stopping the tape.

"Where?" I slammed on the brakes, looking ahead and all around. Wheels screamed on the street around us as we skidded left, then right. Horns blared their opinions of my maneuver. We came to a stop under a large neon sign that blinked yellow and red. I looked at Frank. He was holding his forehead with one hand. The shining top of his hairless head changed colors with the neon sign.

"What the hell?" he said. "You nearly put me through the dashboard. What's going on?"

"You said he was there!"

"Where?"

"I don't know."

"Who?"

I didn't answer. I could not trust myself to be civil.

"You nitwit," said Frank. He leaned back in his seat. "Not out there, there, on the tape—the music. Listen."

He leaned forward and rewound the tape a short way. I heard the crescendo again, and the break, then the two melodies, one older, one new, and more insistent.

"That's Jerry," said Frank. "Mack's son. He's operational now, and I think I understand some things."

"I'm glad you do."

"Let's go. We're blocking traffic. Turn right at the next light."

"Where are we going now, Elmer?"

"I do not look like Elmer Fudd."

"But you think you're James Bond."

"I prefer to model myself on Sydney Reilly. He broke the Trust."

I stopped in mid-chuckle when I remembered Reilly's fate.

"I will not get myself shot," said Frank.

"How do you do that?" I demanded. "How do you read my mind?"

"Logic. You'll catch on pretty soon. By the way, there is some question as to whether old Felix had Reilly executed or managed to turn him."

"I heard that theory," I said. "Which is worse?"

Frank did not answer me. Instead, he laughed.

"I'm sorry," I said, "but I can't follow this. I thought the subject was pretty grim."

He waved at me as he fought to catch his breath. "Turn left on 87th," he said. "I suddenly had a vision of what Mack must have looked like when Samantha asked him if he was gay. And then...." He laughed again, louder. "Then he's offered lessons in etiquette by this little bourgeois American." His chuckle died down. "It's nice to know there are still a few things to laugh about."

He pointed me around the corner onto 87th Street. "Character is the key, my friend," he said. "I've spent more than a decade learning everything I could about them. So I can predict what they'll do and when. I can prevent tragedy. I can get them to work for us. I can manipulate them. Now they are manipulating me and it's hard to take, especially since I'm not sure what's at the end of it."

"I thought you told me we don't control them; we just babysit."

"Not control, manipulate. There's a big difference. Manipulation is more subtle and depends on information. It requires a thorough knowledge of the subject. After fifteen years, it seems they know me better than I know them."

"You seem to know them pretty well," I said. "You've accurately uncovered every move they made, even the details, including who did Mack's laundry. You said that was in character. How did you know to ask?"

"I know him. What have I told you about him so far?"

"That he is abrasive and insulting."

"Did I forget arrogant?"

"Yes, but I figured it out."

"Well, add that to the list. He's insufferably arrogant. I would expect him to have that little old lady waiting on him hand and foot."

"He's thoroughly reprehensible, is he?"

"Thoroughly."

"Then why do you like him?"

When he answered, he formed the words slowly. "I don't know." We rolled down 87th in silence until he said, "Turn right at the next street."

I turned the car down a dark residential street, lined on both sides by neat, boxlike brick houses. A thin layer of wet snow covered the short lawns. Most of the front windows showcased Christmas trees with lights. More lights blinked from eaves and trees, some multicolored, some bright white. I pulled over where Frank told me to.

"A couple of things bother me," he said.

"Only a couple? What are they?"

"First, of course, is Jerry. I don't know him, so I can't tell when he's acting differently. You see, it's the differences that reveal what's going on. The puzzles make me discover reasons. Reasons help me predict what's going to happen next. There are a lot of changes in this operation, and Jerry is a major one."

"But you know the other two men."

"Yes."

"Are there differences?"

"Several important ones." He paused as a car passed us. It was not a Mercedes. We both sighed.

"Mack is taking some massive risks," Frank continued. "To be unsafe for so long is not like him. They must be dead tired, spending the bulk of the past few months alone and exposed. The reason has to be compelling. If they are working for the Soviets, as I suspect we will find out tonight at Rick's, the reason must truly be a whopper. Mack's hatred of communists is almost pathological. I suspect it may be personal."

"You said they were on the back rotor."

"The what?"

"The back rotor of the chopper."

"Did I? Oh. Yeah."

"But you don't know their ideology?"

"No. After all these years, I still don't know."

"So you don't know if they're enemies or allies?"

"I suppose you can call them allies," he said, "but don't confuse it with friends the way Turner has. People who share the same enemies are not necessarily friends. They are our allies for the time being. We'd be foolish not to use them in our interests, and even more foolish to trust them more than that."

I waited for him to go on. The car was getting cold. I did not know where the Mercedes was and I was hungry. I thought we should move. Frank started talking again.

"The Frenchman bothers me," he said. "What could have compelled him to spend even one night in that filthy apartment? And why there, when there was a pretty girl in the more strategic flat? Especially after Jerry's half-hearted attempt failed. And why did that fail? That's another question. But let's stick to Louis. Why did he leave the pretty girl alone? I assure you, it's not like him."

"You want some brainstorming?" I asked.

"Yes. I'm weathered out."

"Maybe she was a watcher."

"No way. They'd have taken her out. She would have blown the whole operation."

"Maybe he didn't leave her alone."

Frank was silent.

"Maybe she lied to us," I continued. "Or, no, not lied, but just didn't tell us. He might have made her promise not to say anything, or...."

"Brilliant," Frank interrupted. "Brilliant. Pardon me while I pat myself on the back for my superb judgment in picking you for this job. You're quite right. She didn't tell us. We've been pointed in one direction and we've trundled along, waiting for somebody to turn us down the right road instead of reading the signposts for ourselves."

"Let's go back and talk to her," I said. I was thinking about hot coffee.

"We can't. No time."

"She may know something."

"Of course, she knows something, or Louis would not have bothered to keep it from us. But it can't be too critical, or they would have killed her or scared her into leaving."

"So they put a temporary stop on the information, knowing you'd figure it out?" I asked.

"It looks that way."

"Then what?"

"Then what what?" He blew on his frozen fingers. "Turn the heat back on. It's cold in here."

"Then what do they expect you to do now that you know?"

"What do you mean?"

I couldn't keep the irritation out of my voice. "If you can predict what they will do based on your knowledge of them," I said slowly, "surely they can do the same. What do they expect from you?"

Frank took a minute to answer. "They expect me to leave it at that."

"Why?"

"Because the information she has is a minor puzzle piece. It's probably only a pillow talk revelation of some sort they don't want me to know. I am pressured by time and fear not to seek it out. I could go back later. If there is a later."

"But not now?"

"No."

"Then they are manipulating you. The babysitter is being babysat."

"Yes. Damn it."

"There's no way we have time?" I wanted badly to get out of there. I checked my door lock again, and the mirrors.

"Only if we skip dinner."

This was a subject near and dear to my heart. The bread-sticks at lunch were long gone.

"Would they expect you to skip dinner?" I asked.

"I don't miss many meals."

I remembered passing a restaurant on 87th Street.

"I'm not going to let Mack think he can read my mind every time," said Frank vehemently. "Let's go talk to the girl. To hell with dinner."

The only welcome part of this news was that we were leaving. I put the car in gear.

Frank put his hand on the wheel. "Wait. Not yet. We're here for a reason. I have something to tell you. Turn off the engine."

I did as I was told and waited, not with much patience.

"Are you absolutely sure," he said, "That they did not mark this car until after you got to it?"

"Yes."

"And nothing has been out of place at your hotel?"

"Nothing." I remembered the man next door to Charlie, but the thought was driven out of my head by the Mercedes that drove by slowly.

My misery was complete when the Mercedes parked down the street and no one got out.

"You're sure, Steve?" said Frank softly. "They must not hear what I have to tell you. Are you absolutely sure?"

FOURTEEN

It was like flying in weather. I had to rely on instruments, not instinct. There was no Mercedes on that street when I got there. "Yes," I said. "I'm sure. This car is secure."

"Any theories?" he asked.

"No." I was not interested in theories, only flight, of the save my skin variety, not the soar my soul.

"Then I will tell you my theory." Frank took a breath, puffed out his cheeks, and began, "I base it on the one person I know best."

"Mack?"

"No. Me. I have to ask myself, what makes me do the things I do? There are many reasons. Sometimes fear is one of them, but as uncomfortable as I am with the knowledge that our friends are sitting with possibly unfriendly intentions a few yards up the road from us, my fear at this moment is not the laser-burning kind that sears the heart. As much as I hate to see that car here, there is another place where its appearance would make me crazy."

I understood what he was talking about. Portraits of his wife, seven children, and two grandchildren adorned a bookcase in his office. I thought of my own family and shuddered.

"Exactly," he said, registering my shiver.

"But they don't have families," I said without thinking.

"On the contrary, my friend. They do. Jerry is one."

"He's grown."

"He mentioned a younger sister."

"Dead."

"My point exactly."

I picked up the line of Frank's reasoning. "Mack said he had a wife but lost her."

"And if you were to fail to prevent the unthinkable, what would move you to act then?"

"Rache," I said. "Revenge."

Frank nodded. "Now I will tell you a story. Look at the house on our right."

I looked. There was a light in the window. The curtains were drawn. No decorations.

"The light is on a timer," Frank explained. "No one lives there. The man who used to live there died eight months ago and his daughter has not yet disposed of the property. The man was known to us as Fred."

I had heard the name. "Fred from our office? Your old boss? Babysitter for the elder Sobieski?"

"Right, right, and triple right. And his daughter Alex married the younger Sobieski."

"In Chicago?"

"My question exactly. Not the marriage. I was here; it's a fact. They met on an operation. Very romantic. No, since we got the FBI message yesterday, my question has been, 'Why Chicago?' I think there must be a connection. It's not pure coincidence. They could have cleaned up Jared's network one at a time in different cities. They could have set the trap for him anywhere. Why here?"

"Because Jared's family is here," I answered.

"Precisely."

"How could anyone kill a child like Janey?"

"How indeed? I don't know the answer to that, but I know the answer to why. Children grow up to be like their parents. Some people have enemies who hate them not only for what they do but for who they are. Some people live in a room with no windows. Others don't even have any doors. I told you that once, didn't I?"

"Yes."

"I told Jello that once, too. Right here on this street, I explained that to him and I told him that I had no intention of entering that room. I have a hard enough time living without windows."

He paused and shivered. The car was getting cold again.

"Eight months ago, Fred died unexpectedly," he continued. "He had given me the means to contact his daughter, Alex, in an emergency. His wife died a few years ago and there was no one else. I prepared the message to Alex, but Stupid Directive of the Month à la Jello was that he was the only one who could sign messages, so I was forced to show it to him. He wanted to delay sending it so we could go through the house. I told him that wouldn't be necessary; I had a crew in the house already, and they would be out of there well before Alex arrived. That was not good enough. He insisted we come out here and see it for ourselves. We sent the message before we left for Chicago, but we put a delay on the visas to hold them up."

"They all came?" I asked.

"No. Just her."

"But didn't you say she was an American?"

"No, I didn't. She was, or is, but you've fallen into the trap of making assumptions without verification. The visas were for her bodyguards. She had six of them to protect her when she finally arrived, mad as a wet hen over the delay. Before she got here, we managed to spend two days in that house. We went through everything twice, tore out suspect walls, and used x-ray equipment. There were no letters, no addresses, no contacts. Nothing. Fred knew better. He was a professional and never wrote anything down. We put the house back together and prepared to leave."

"Another Jello-inspired rat screw?" I said.

"No," said Frank. His voice had become quiet. "He was right. There was something there and we would not have found it if I had not gone personally to take a look. I noticed something about the little bar Fred had in the living room. There were three kinds of vodka, which fit because Fred's favorite drink was vodka tonic. I am perhaps the only one still around who could remember that. Anyway, there was a refrigerator in the bar, one of those little square jobs that hold a couple of six-packs and some ice. I opened it again, just as the searchers had done. It was turned off and had been off for some time because it was dry and empty. I looked inside carefully, no sign of anything, but why was it empty? I looked in the main refrigerator in the kitchen. There were three bottles of tonic water."

"Maybe the little one in the bar was broken."

"Maybe. I took it apart to see if I could fix it."

"And you found?"

"A photo album." Frank's voice was now completely hushed, his manner subdued. "It was a slim album about eight by nine inches that slipped perfectly between the inner lining and outer casing where the insulation had been re-moved. The door seal buttoned over it."

I wiped the fog off the windshield so I could see out. Nothing moved.

"The photos featured the same little girl at different ages," continued Frank, "starting when she was a baby until about age eleven. One picture, though, had more people in it. It had a date of a few years ago written on the back. The people were grouped in front of a Christmas tree. There was a fireplace to their right, open boxes, and torn wrappings on the floor around them. The little girl was about two and she sat in the lap of a woman that it broke my heart to know I'd never meet. She was beautiful, and so was the other little girl of about four who sat on her right, obviously her daughter. There was an adolescent boy on the woman's left, with his arm around her shoulder. He held a guitar with a ribbon around it."

"Who were they?" I asked.

Frank looked ahead where there was nothing to see but the frost on the windshield. I think he forgot I was there. He went on talking. "I knew what I was looking at. The main subject of the album had to be Fred's granddaughter, Sobieski's daughter. The others I couldn't be sure about. The woman was not Alex, but the boy with the guitar reminded me of Mack. Jello noticed the resemblance, too, and decided we would keep a couple of pictures. I told him that was dangerous and unnecessary. I would remember their faces. He said we were required to keep records. I told him that if Charlemagne ever found out we had these...."

He paused and I wiped the windshield again. "I explained to Jello," he began again after a deep breath, "as patiently as I could, that while Charlemagne's families were probably protected by a fortress of expensive security, their ultimate defense was also the only thing that protected my own family—their anonymity. I never wanted to enter Charlemagne's room without doors. I do not have the skill to survive in their world."

"What did Jello say then?" I asked after a long pause.

"He said if I didn't want Charlemagne to find out we had the pictures, I damn-well better not tell them. We took the group photo and one recent picture of the little girl. That was when Jello restricted access to the file to just the two of us. I haven't touched it since. I don't want my fingerprints on it, to tell you the truth."

"How old would the boy be now?" I asked, doing a few calculations of my own.

"In his early twenties."

I started the engine and turned on the heat. "Is that all? Can we get out of here?" I asked.

"Yes."

We drove slowly past the Mercedes. Its windows were fogged. I wanted to pound on one of them and scream "What do you want?" I was hungry and tired and afraid, and to tell the truth, Charlemagne was the least of my fears.

"Jerry must have been taught English by Sobieski's wife," I said after I negotiated a left turn across three lanes of traffic on 87th Street.

"Yes," said Frank. "It sounds like he speaks flawless American English. He must have a better ear than his father."

"Mack isn't good with languages?"

"That depends on what you call good. He's fluent in six or seven languages. Besides his native German, his best is Russian, but pronunciation is a struggle for him; it's always accented."

"It's nice to know there's something he doesn't do well."

"Oh, he's human. He makes a mistake from time to time, but when he does, it's on the side of caution. When you meet him, assuming we all come out of this healthy—let's be optimists—he will probably insult you and then grill you on every detail of the commission you're offering, the most critical being the verification."

"I wonder if we went through a drive-through," I said, to hide the growling from my stomach, "if the Mercedes would follow us through."

"It's still there, eh?"

He wasn't taking the hint. I was going to go hungry.

"Frank," I said after a few minutes.

"Yes."

"I think you should give back the photos."

"I can't."

"Why not?"

"Unlike Jay Turner, I know who I work for. Uncle Sam signs my paycheck, not Charlemagne."

"It isn't right, Frank."

"Now hold on, Steve," said Frank heatedly. "Don't start deciding right and wrong again. Choose between allowed and not allowed, feasible and infeasible, expedient and inexpedient, but never right and wrong. That is a moral labyrinth you'll never leave."

"Okay, Frank," I said. "But give them back the photos. It is allowed because Jello is away, leaving you in charge. You make the rules now. It is feasible because it will be no problem contacting them since they are right behind us. Finally, it is, in my junior, amateur, unschooled opinion, expedient because my junior, amateur, unschooled instinct tells me they know you have them and they want them back."

"Instinct is not verifiable in this case, my dear chap. Give me some other basis. If they want the pictures, why don't they ask?"

"Your revenge theory is one basis for my instinct," I said. "And two minor facts that I think are suggestive. As for asking you for them, how would you answer?"

"No," said Frank. "It would be disloyal. I can't be disloyal."

"Disloyal to what, Frank?"

He did not answer. I pulled over in front of the pizza parlor on 105th Street.

"Disloyal to Jello?" I asked, turning off the engine. "You can fire me right now, Frank, but I am loyal to the Constitution, not to Jello."

"Your superiors have access to a wider range of information than you do, my friend," said Frank. "Be careful about the standards you decide to change at your whim."

"Yes. I know that argument," I said. "You're right: I don't have the fucking big picture, only a small piece of it. In that piece I see an idiot, or worse, making an idiotic decision that may have killed four innocent people and almost killed two more. I know how to fucking follow orders. I have learned that's no excuse."

"Steve, to fight these people...."

"I will not become one of them, Frank."

During the long silence that followed, I waited for Frank to send me home.

"So what are the facts that make you so sure they know about the photos?" Frank said finally.

"I'm not all that sure," I answered, still prepared for unemployment. "I said it's only a theory. But I'm thinking of the dark room in the apartment where the three were killed."

"There were no pictures there."

"Exactly."

"And the second fact?"

"No matter how secure the section vault may be, no matter how thick the walls, no matter how often the combination is changed, it is still administered by people. Access to that file may be limited to two, but it's controlled by dozens."

We spent another few minutes with our own thoughts until Frank broke the silence.

"Drive back down Michigan Avenue," he said, "and stop at the first gas station you see with a phone booth. I need to make a couple of calls."

I waited in the car, watching Frank on the phone, watching the traffic for signs of Charlemagne. One of Frank's calls seemed animated. He was arguing. The argument resolved, he hung up looking satisfied. When he came back to the car, he pointed out to me that the Mercedes was parked in a vacant lot across the street.

"The minute we leave this car," he said, "we'll have to assume it's compromised. Tomorrow morning, before we start, I want you to turn this one in and get another one. Make sure you pick out the new one. Don't let the rental agency pick it for you."

He leaned back in his seat as we returned to Edbrooke Avenue and parked again in front of the pizza parlor. "You know," he said, talking to the ceiling, "the revenge theory doesn't take into account the Soviet connection. And as for your photo theory, there may be some pictures involved somewhere, but it cannot be the ones Jello and I took. He and I were the only people who knew we had them until I told you just now."

"He may have told somebody."

"No. Jello never tells anybody anything—I take that back. He never tells them what they need to know. He always keeps the wrong secrets, but he always keeps them."

"What about his special project?" I asked. "The one he bragged about to you?"

Frank didn't say anything, so I pursued the subject.

"When you contacted Charlemagne eight months ago and they laughed at you and walked out, did you tell them Jello had the verification, or that your boss had it?"

"I said my boss had it."

"How did they know Jello was your boss?"

Frank remained silent.

"I have another question, Frank."

"Go ahead, I'm listening."

"Does Jello know you're getting his job?"

"I don't think so. Why?"

"If he knew, would he be happy for you, or would he hate you?"

"He already hates me, Steve. What are you getting at?" He sat up abruptly. "No. You're wrong. If Jello set me up and I'm the target, then what the hell are they waiting for? Answer me that, eh?"

I answered: "Verification."

FIFTEEN

We parked in front of the pizza parlor. I wanted pizza; Frank wanted information. I suspected only one of us would get what he wanted, and since Frank was the boss.... I followed him into the shop like a puppy follows a stranger hoping for a biscuit.

The proprietor of Geno's Real Italian Pizzas was a solemn, harried man of about forty, very much in charge and not interested in fools. He introduced himself as Joshua Atkinson and wiped off pizza dough onto a towel tucked in his belt before shaking hands with us. He was very tall, well over six feet, and looked like he worked out. A lot. I wondered what his style was and decided it was Aikido because he moved like a tiger. Two scars, keloid and yellow, snaked over otherwise regular features on his brown face, like warrior lines. It made him look fierce.

"Go ahead and ask," he said in response to Frank's polite request, "but I have to keep working. The guy who helps me disappeared again and I'm on my own."

"Again? He's disappeared before?"

"Yeah. Undependable S.O.B."

"Do you remember when that was?"

Frank did not get an answer right away. Atkinson pulled a pizza from the oven, boxed it, and marked it.

"Is he the guy you're asking about? The Cajun?"

Frank nodded. "Can you tell me when he disappeared on you the first time?"

"In October." He spread dough over an empty pan. "His girlfriend across the street can tell you. The day after he left, his old girlfriend went after her with acid. Naass-tee. I imagine she'll know the exact day."

"Old girlfriend?"

"Yeah. The one they pulled out feet first yesterday." He pointed a floured finger at the building across the street and then at Frank. "You cops? You think Emile killed her?"

"No, we're not cops," said Frank.

"But you think he killed her." Atkinson put the new pizza in the oven.

I found it strange the way he did it, like a shrug standing in for passion. Slide pizza into oven, slide corpse out of building, natural partners to conversation.

"I wouldn't be surprised if he did kill her," he said matter-of-factly. "He had plenty of reason. She was gross, and nothin' but trouble."

Plenty of reason. I kept my mouth shut and tried to shake off this infectious indifference to a life.

"I threw her out of here a couple of times," Atkinson continued. "I don't know why Emile ever took up with her in the first place, but it didn't surprise me when he dumped her as soon as the new girl came."

Frank winced. He covered it with another question.

"Tell me, Mr. Atkinson, have you ever been robbed?"

The man grinned. "I don't have much trouble with that. If you mean has anybody been stupid enough to try it, the answer's yeah. Once. Back in August."

"What happened?"

He pulled a pizza, round, gold, steaming, born to be eaten, from the oven. Not that I cared. I listened to the interview. Of course.

"Emile had just pulled one out of the oven," Atkinson was saying. "Like this one." He swayed slightly and with him the pizza on its long-handled spatula, threatening to hypnotize me. "A guy came in." He grinned. "He said gimme all you got and Emile…."

He swung the pizza sideways through the air, swiftly, deftly, so that it did not slide off the spatula. I ducked involuntarily. I had been closest to the simulated line of fire.

Atkinson's expression turned grim. "The guy ran out screaming. I guess the cheese burned his face pretty bad. I met somebody like that once." He pointed at the scar across his face.

Frank opened his mouth to ask another question, but he was talking again. "Emile went around the counter and picked up the weapon the guy dropped. He took it to pieces, put it back together, and put it in the cash drawer. He figured it wasn't registered and might come in handy—just in case. It's still there; you want it?"

"No. Thanks." Frank looked at that pizza. So did I. "Is there anything else about him you can tell us?" he asked.

Atkinson weighed his response. "What's to know? The girls liked him. He made good pizzas, and when he showed up, he worked hard. What else?"

"What did you think of him?"

The huge man looked Frank directly in the eye while he answered. "I think if he's a Cajun, I'm a Swede. I don't know who he was, but I know what he was, and if you're not a cop, I know what you are, too. I was in the game in Southeast Asia. I ain't stupid. I know when to mind my own business, which is what I did when he was here, and what I'm gonna continue to do. Any more questions?"

"No. Thank you for your time, Mr. Atkinson."

"My pleasure, Mr. Cardova." The phone rang. He answered it, "Yeah?" as we walked out the door.

We slipped across the street. I don't mean we made our way unobtrusively to the apartment building like good secret squirrels. I mean we slipped. The temperature had dropped quickly after sunset, freezing the wet snow on the old humpback side street, where layers of asphalt were piled on top of each other for so many years that the middle, where the paving was thickest, was two feet higher than the gutters. Getting to the middle was not easy, an uphill climb without purchase on solid ice. Coming down the other side was quicker and sportier. I slid to the curb. Frank followed, his arms waving wildly for balance, shouting "Whoa!" and a few other words.

"Now that I've provided the entertainment for the evening," he said when he was safely in the doorway, "I wish they'd pack up and go home."

"Where are they?" I searched the street.

"To your left on the other side of the street, about fifty yards down. It's just outside the circle of light from the street lamp."

"I see it."

Frank's face was pinched and scowling. "I hate it," he said, "when there are no windows. I can't see out, and I don't know who's looking in."

"But without windows," I said, "they can't look in."

"You think so?"

This time, it was a slower, harder climb to the third floor than it had been first thing in the morning. We were rewarded, though, by a cup of hot coffee from Sarah Tisdale.

Frank and I sipped reverently, hunching over and around the steaming mugs, selfishly trying to consume every vapor, every warm, overactive molecule. Sarah sat on a cushion opposite us, pulling tissues from a box labeled generically, black on white. She blew her nose and dried a fresh tear, then smiled at me—us.

"Sarah, why are you crying?" Frank asked when he had thawed.

She didn't answer.

"Is it because he's gone?" he persisted.

"Yes!"

We waited for the end of another crying fit.

"Did he tell you to be out of the apartment yesterday?" Frank asked. "Or did somebody else tell you?"

"He said not to tell you anything." There was more doubt than fear in her expression, though there was plenty of that, too.

"I know he told you that, Sarah. I've worked with him for a long time and I know him very well. You can tell me."

"Have you seen him?"

"In a manner of speaking, yes."

"I miss him so bad!" She sobbed again.

"Did he tell you to stay away from here yesterday?"

"Yes."

Frank's smile was a little self-satisfied.

"Can you tell me how you met him?" he asked.

"I told you this morning," she said. "That was the truth. He said to stick to the truth. 'Keep it simple,' he said. 'And let him draw his own conclusions.'"

"Yes, well, you did that very well, Sarah. Now tell me when and how you two, uh, formed a relationship."

She blew her nose. "It was the night we all went out together when Jerry and I didn't hit it off. I came home and went to bed. Emile must have gone to work. I don't know how he got in. I once asked him if he had a key, but he didn't answer me. I know I never gave him a key."

"That night," Frank prodded.

"That night I was asleep. He sat down on my bed and woke me up. It was after midnight. I wasn't really surprised to see him; I had a feeling all during dinner. I even thought Emile was glad Jerry and I didn't get along."

Sarah paused again when she noticed my cup was empty. I ignored the impatient look Frank gave me and accepted the offer of a refill. She offered Frank a cup of chamomile tea, telling him it would help him relax. He managed to convince her that coffee would suit him better and sat fidgeting on his cushion until she came back with two coffees and a chamomile tea. She made him taste the tea and smiled at me.

"You were telling us about when you and Emile...," he said.

"Yes. Emile said, 'Mind if I join you?' and I said, 'You smell like pizza.'" Sarah smiled into her tea cup. "And he said, 'You smell like a woman.'"

After a short, smiling silence, she looked up at Frank and said: "Did you want details?"

"Uh, no." The question seemed to startle him. "What about the last time you saw him?" he asked, collecting himself.

"Friday night." She paused as new tears appeared in her eyes. "He told me he was leaving and wouldn't be back.

That's when he told me not to be here yesterday. I begged him not to go. He was always straight with me. Told me in the beginning this wasn't permanent or anything, but you always agree to these things before you get attached, you know. So I told him about Dottie, and like, he was furious with me for not telling him before. I never seen him so mad."

"What about Dottie?"

"Well, I told you how jealous she was didn't I?"

We nodded.

"In October, Emile left for a few days. I didn't know if he'd be back or not, but Dottie must have figured he was gone for good. The day after he left, I came out my door to go to the store. I needed something sweet—I get this incredible, like, sweet tooth sometimes—and she was waiting for me in the hall, holding this bottle. She like, threw it right at my face. I ducked, but it went all over my shoulder, up my neck and it was acid. It hurt like hell. See?" She stretched the neck of her sweatshirt and showed us what once must have been a lovely shoulder, now badly scarred and still partly bandaged.

"Then Emile came back," she continued, "and he had a fit. He must have said some things to Dottie that scared her pretty bad because she stayed away from me for a while. But about November, I started getting these phone calls. At first, she called about once a week and didn't say who she was, just screamed hateful stuff. But by the beginning of this month, she came right out with it."

Sarah took a long sip of tea. I noticed her hand was shaking.

"What did she say?" Frank asked.

"She said she was going to kill me as soon as Emile left. She called every day and told me that. I was scared. But I didn't tell him because I was scared of her. I wanted him to stay. Do you understand?"

"Yes," said Frank softly. "What did Emile say when you told him about the phone calls?"

"When he cooled off, he said not to worry; he'd take care of it." Sarah looked at Frank. "I didn't know he was going to kill her. Honest."

"I believe you. Did you ever notice his gun?"

She stared at Frank wide-eyed. "You are cops. I don't want to get him in trouble."

"We're not cops. If anybody's in trouble, it's me."

Frank put his mug down on the floor beside him and leaned forward. "I'm trying to understand why he went to the trouble to tell you not to talk to me. Nobody else was briefed that way. What do you know that was important enough to keep from me?" He asked the next question before she had a chance to answer. "Did you ever touch his gun?"

"Oh no! He warned me again and again never to go near it."

"That's a first," muttered Frank.

"Excuse me?"

"Try to remember, Sarah." Frank seemed to be trying to remember something himself. He squinted, pulling thin lids over his round eyes. "Did he say anything unusual or puzzling? Did he talk about his family? His friends?"

"He was always unusual," she said smiling. "He never mentioned any family. Once I asked him what happened to Jerry, and he said he'd gone home, if that's any help?"

"When was that?"

"Shortly after we started going out. Jerry came back though. I saw him. I told you that, didn't I?"

Frank nodded and stared at the floor in front of him, still squinting, willing her memory to work.

"Emile had a best friend," Sarah said after a long pause.

Frank's eyes opened, popping, as his head came up. "He did?"

"Yes. He said he had a best friend. I never met him though."

"What did he say about his best friend?"

Sarah seemed reluctant to answer and took another slow sip of tea before speaking. "I told him once that I love him. It must have been sometime after he came back in October because I still had all the bandages." She spoke slowly. "I knew better. He was always real honest about it being temporary, but I had to tell him. He didn't look at me, only at the ceiling, and told me not to talk nonsense. I put my head on his shoulder and pulled his arm around me tighter, and I told him love was not nonsense. He argued it was, and still wouldn't look at me. He'd seen his best friend crying over a coffin, he said, and that was never going to happen to him. He was so serious. It kinda broke the spell that morning. He got dressed and left without saying anything else. I kept things the way he wanted after that—temporary and fun."

"Bingo," whispered Frank. He looked at me sideways.

"I'm sorry I couldn't help you," she said.

"You've been a great help, Sarah," said Frank. "Thank you."

"You're welcome. Are you out of trouble now?"

...

I did not ask him the same question when we walked out into the cold. The Mercedes was still across the street, beyond the light.

SIXTEEN

"So why is it about time Louis told Sarah to stay away from his gun?" I asked Frank as I drove us to Rick's for the appointment with Slavin.

"What?" Frank shook himself and straightened up a bit in his seat. "Oh, Louis has a nasty habit of not warning women and then shooting them when they reach toward his gun in the heat of the moment."

"He does what?"

"He shoots them."

I waited for more explanation. The puny portion of confidence I had built in the last few hours was gone. Frank crumpled back into his corner, not interested in talking. I was interested, though.

"Is this fact?" I asked. "I mean, do you know of it actually happening? How many times?"

"Twice that I know of." Frank yawned, wide and noisy.

"That you know? It happened on your watch?"

"Once. The other time it happened to somebody else. I don't have any details of that one. Not verified."

"But what happened? Don't you think this is something I should know about?" The last word reached an octave over my normal speaking voice.

Frank did not hide the irritation in his voice. He spoke quickly, demanding with his tone, if not with the actual words, that I drop the subject.

"Operations are usually short and uncomplicated, Steve, but when they go on for more than a couple of days, the Frenchman, and maybe the others, but definitely the Frenchman, will find a little amusement along the way. Your job will be to check her bona fides and make sure she is warned not to get too curious. On my fourth operation with them, I failed to do both. She was on her own operation. I don't know who she was working for. These guys have too many enemies to count anyway. She was well-equipped to do the job but got dramatic about it and reached for his gun. He got to it first. Simple. They've never taken my word about the bona fides of a girl since."

"But this time?"

"This time he warned Sarah. I suppose it's not surprising since if he lost her, he'd be back across the hall. I've never known him to be so careful with a girl before, though."

"What do you do when…?"

"Turn left at the next light and let me think for a while."

He gave directions for parking the car, not for dealing with disaster. We walked to our meeting at Rick's.

"Any sign of the Mercedes?" he asked, blowing on his hands as if his breath would somehow make all the difference against the insidious cold.

"None." I tried to watch the cloud my breath made in the cold air under a street light overhead, but Frank was setting such a fast pace that it was behind me almost as soon as I spoke. It was like leaving a word behind on that empty street, first warm and living, then frozen, now dissolved.

"The car's probably wired by now," Frank said to me over his shoulder. "They don't need to follow us anymore."

"I didn't think what we talked about would be anything new to them," I said defensively, trotting three steps to keep up. I never understood how such a short, round man could move so quickly without actually running.

"I agree," he said. "I just needed time to think about your picture theory. Sarah's bit of information reinforces it, don't you think? I mean, if Mack is Louis' best friend, and if the coffin he cried over held the woman in that picture Jello and I kept, then if the picture had anything to do with her death, anybody who had anything to do with the picture is in deep trouble. I can see that. But I didn't do anything with it but lock it in a vault. The only other person who would know what to do with it and have access to it at the same time is such a blithering idiot that it blows your whole theory."

"How's that?" I squeezed the words out in frozen gasps.

"Setting me up is far too subtle a move for Jello. He could never think of it, let alone pull it off."

"But if he did?"

"He didn't."

"But if he did, Frank," I insisted. "If he did then he's not such an idiot."

"That is not worth considering."

"It is worth considering, Frank. It's always a possibility."

"I refuse to believe it. I told you before; it's impossible."

At that time I knew only the popular history of Frank and Jello, the stories told in the section of political maneuvers and dogmatic wrangling and loud, public arguments in vehement words that left them both red and shaking. If I had any sense, I would have realized such emotional hatreds have emotional beginnings.

Only recently somebody told me about their exploits as advisors in Southeast Asia, when they were brothers in arms, friends depending on each other for survival. It took me more serious thought, several months too late, to realize what my smug little theory meant to Frank. For Jello to turn would be a betrayal of his country that Frank could never understand. To arrange Frank's death was treachery of the first magnitude, even after twenty-five years of backstabbing competition.

I walked into Rick's without knowing any of this. Puzzled and preoccupied by Frank's blindness, I stumbled over the doorstep into a tray of empty glasses carried by a waitress. The tray flew from her hand over the bar and crashed into a row of bottles along a mirrored wall, announcing our arrival to the roomful of assorted spooks and assassins there gathered.

"Nice touch," Frank said sarcastically.

The waitress didn't care. She smiled and asked for my order. As we stepped into the large room to the right of the bar, I noticed half a dozen men in all three sections putting away their weapons.

"The rules against violence in a sovereign house are enforced by the clientele," Frank explained as we surveyed the left side of the room. "Making too much noise here can be unhealthy; I wouldn't make a habit of it if I were you."

I kept my mouth shut.

"There's Slavin," said Frank nodding toward the second table along the left wall.

"How do you know?"

"He's got a bag from Just Jeans."

"For the black market back home?"

"Of course not. He's a member of the Soviet aristocracy—the nomenklatura—central committee, inner circle KGB. He doesn't need the black market. But he can't go home to his wife and kids without some American blue jeans any more than I could come home from Hong Kong without a string of freshwater pearls and assorted jade earrings."

"Just like us, is he?" I asked.

"No way," Frank whispered through his teeth. "Don't ever make that mistake. Anything we have in common with these people is on the most basic human level only. Don't let that confuse you. They do not think like us. They speak the same words, like peace and freedom, but their definitions are something else, something appalling and terrifying. Their privileges are built on those definitions. Make no mistake, my friend. This man is the enemy. Don't let the blue jeans give him a benign camouflage."

I watched Frank, shocked by his intensity. He stared at the Russian on the left.

"Us Against Them?" I asked, not knowing what it was I wanted to know.

He nodded, scowling. It was an answer of sorts. To Frank, this was war, a personal battle where the stakes were bigger than the lives of the combatants. He was locked into it, hating perfectly, for a higher reason I didn't quite grasp.

But he held it tight and prepared to meet his enemy face to face. He tensed each limb and released, like an athlete at a meet. The muscles over his cheeks and around his mouth were pulled tight. He looked grim and strangely young and oddly exuberant. This was his moment. This was THE battle.

"And when you've defeated him, Frank? What will you do then?"

He shuddered, shook himself, and looked at me. "Go on to the next one. There will never be a shortage, my boy. Don't you worry. They're everywhere. I told you that before.

Over here we call 'em the Mob. Over there, the Party." He grinned or tried to, but the scowl would not let go of his face; it only retreated behind a jolly mask.

"Another reason I know that's Slavin," Frank said, still stretching that odd grin, "is by the way all the local bad guys are fawning all over him trying to get close. Look at them. I wonder why they don't bow."

I was watching Frank, but I knew Slavin had noticed us. I could feel his stare.

"And finally, I know it's him," said Frank, "because I recognize him from a picture on file in the vault. Let's go say hi."

I didn't smile back at the joke. I didn't have that much control.

Ignaty Mikhailovich Slavin did not shake hands with us. He dismissed his hangers-on with an impatient gesture, cleared the tables around us with another gesture, and pointed to the two seats in front of him. After unsuccessful attempts to communicate in English and Russian, we settled on German, the only language all three of us knew.

"What's your brief and who gave it to you?" Frank began.

"Charlemagne gave it, but there is a price." The Russian's face was stretched in a sneer.

"Name it," said Frank.

"Verification that Jared is dead." The sneer seemed permanent.

"Saw him myself last night, in a drawer at the morgue. He didn't even complain about the cold—must have been acclimated by all those Moscow winters."

"I do not have time to listen to your infamous jokes," said Slavin. "Ask your questions and I will see if I can answer them."

The waitress brought the drinks Frank and I had ordered. Slavin asked for another vodka.

Frank did not touch his drink. "Who commissioned it?"

"We did."

Though he was surely bursting with questions. Frank was cautious, pausing between each one, trying to gather as much information as he could without giving away his own line of reasoning.

The first question was simply, "Why?"

"He was out of control," said Slavin. "Seriously out of control. He was involved in something that is a threat to Soviet state security."

"What?"

"I cannot tell you. But I can say that it is not important to this case."

"It resulted in his death," said Frank.

"But it has nothing to do with your own," replied Slavin.

Frank's pause was longer than usual. "Why are you telling me this?" he asked finally.

"This is part of the price. I cannot believe you Americans pay such extortionist fees. Surely a few simple revolutionaries cannot be worth so much money."

"They are when they threaten millions, you bastard, not to mention civilization itself." Frank hunched his shoulders over the table, still not touching his drink.

"Can we refrain from name-calling?" Slavin said. The waitress placed his vodka in front of him. He drank it in one gulp. "Or is that too difficult for such a civilized bourgeois shithead?"

Everybody felt better after that and we entered round two.

"Let's get back to the price," said Frank, finally sipping his drink. "What else did they charge you?"

"Too much hard currency and a couple of sacrifices."

"Am I part of the commission?"

"Would I spend a ruble on you?"

"Your babysitter's dead, too, you know," said Frank after another, longer sip.

"No, I did not know." Slavin shrugged. "Not much of a loss."

"Not one of your best men?"

"Of course not. I could not compromise one of my best. This entire operation has put me in a difficult position. My only consolation is that yours is worse."

"I'm overwhelmed by your concern," said Frank, leaning forward again. "What, exactly, do you know about my position?"

Slavin stared at Frank for a long time, then looked at the wall on his right. He peeled back a loose piece of wallpaper distractedly and seemed to have no intention of answering, so we were both surprised when he finally spoke. "Not much, I am afraid," he said. "I know I would not like to be Charlemagne's enemy right now, and my intuition tells me that you are considered one."

I dared to break the long pause that followed with a question of my own, not that I had any business doing so, but I could feel Frank's discomfort. I sensed it in his silence. I thought I could distract Slavin while gaining some more information in the bargain. What these two found obvious was still a mystery to me.

"When did you offer them the commission?" I asked.

Slavin examined me before answering. His voice was mechanical. "In January."

"They took it?"

"They refused."

"Why? Did they say?"

"They did not like my verification."

"What did you finally do to convince them?" This was a shot in the dark. I was not sure he would answer.

He stared at me, trying to read my thoughts. He decided (wrongly) that I did not know what I was asking, because, to my surprise, he answered.

"I allowed subsequent events to carry them to their own verification."

"How?"

Slavin accepted my stupid look and put on a patient air as he said, "I gave Jared what he always wanted. The rest followed naturally."

"You gave...." I didn't finish the question, because Frank interrupted.

"And what was it Jared always wanted?" he asked.

"Rache."

SEVENTEEN

T he parking lot at my hotel was not as full as it had been. People were going home for Christmas. Other people. The wino begging for loose change sat propped against the same pillar, grimy fingers grasping the neck of another bottle in a paper sack.

"Merry Christmas," I said, dropping the change from my pockets into the box in front of him. The bum grinned at me, gap-toothed. I shuddered.

The lobby was perfectly silent. The management had spared me even the insipid wilted-leaf holiday music over the intercom system. Blinking lights on the Christmas tree in a corner by the reception desk left a pattern of colored streaks in my streaming eyes. I could barely keep them open. Sleep would be a cinch. I was on my way.

"I owe you, Steve," came a voice behind me. "Let me buy you a drink."

A hand clamped onto my shoulder, making me pull away instinctively. "I've had a drink," I said. "Thanks anyway, Charlie." I blinked at him, trying to focus. His suit was wrinkled, his tie uneven. There was a coffee stain on his shirt. I wondered if I looked as bad.

"You look awful," he said. "I insist. We'll go to the piano bar."

"How about a rain check?" I mumbled. "I'm beat."

"No rain checks. I leave tomorrow. Let's go."

I was too exhausted to resist and followed him meekly into the deserted bar. We sat at a low counter surrounding a white grand piano. A bartender took our order and brought our drinks. Three or four people sat at a table against a far wall. Charlie lifted my spirits but also pestered me. It was tough keeping up with his questions and almost impossible to stick to my legend without contradicting myself. I say almost because somehow, I managed it.

"My dad's a little disappointed with me," he said when the subject had worked its way around to our families. "What about yours?"

"My what?" I took a sip of my gin and tonic, convinced that one more drop of alcohol would surely make me unconscious. It didn't though.

"Your dad," said Charlie. "Is he happy with what you're doing?"

"He's dead. Died a few years ago."

"I think sometimes parents make unrealistic plans for their kids, don't you?"

"Huh?"

"What did your dad want you to do?"

"He wanted me to be a pilot," I said, studying the lemon in my glass.

"And you are one. Was he pleased?"

"I was one. And yes, he was pleased."

"Was? What happened?"

"I had an accident. So why is your dad disappointed with you?" I was desperate to change the subject.

"He sent me to very good music schools and finds it hard to accept that I'll never be a professional musician."

"Why?" I asked. "Don't you want to?"

"I can't."

"Why not?"

"I just can't."

"So you sell tractors instead? You don't look like a musician." I studied his conservative haircut and rumpled business suit.

"What's a musician supposed to look like?"

"Can you play an instrument?"

"Several."

"What about this one?" I had noticed him eyeing the piano.

His face brightened. "No, I couldn't."

"Come on. Let's hear something. What can you play?"

"What do you want to hear?"

"Do you know any of that classical stuff?"

"Some." Was there irony in that half-smile?

I tried to remember the name of the composer Frank made me listen to in the car. I couldn't. I knew the name sounded like a word that echoed in my head, though, bouncing off the walls of my skull like a blip on a computer screen, looking for brain matter to settle down on and be solved by, to be thought of and processed, sifted and stored, if it weren't for the alcohol.

"The guy I'm thinking of sounds like *Rache*," I said. "I heard a piano concerto by him today. You wouldn't know who I'm talking about, would you?"

Charlie said nothing. He studied me. Then he grinned— a boyish, mischievous, teasing grin that made me forget the penny popping up in the cake. "Rachmaninov," he said. "Is that it?"

"That's it."

"His second?"

"I think so."

"I'll play the first movement."

"Do you know it?"

What a stupid question. He played the first ominous chords and looked at me once to see me nod, yes, this is it. His concentration deepened so that he moved to another planet where communication is based on discreet bits arranged in octaves.

Maybe I was fascinated because I was hearing it live, not from a tape deck. How can any man control his coordination in such an intricate operation as playing a piano? It occurred to me that Charlie was very, very good. Of course, I'm no expert. But this music moved me strangely. There was no question of sleep.

It didn't matter that there was no orchestra. The same power rushed in a torrent to a crescendo that broke out on top with more insistence and distinction than it had on the tape. At that point—the one where I slammed on the brakes and almost broke Frank's bald head—at that point, Charlie looked up at me and grinned, then retreated to his planet and finished the movement.

"I don't understand why you think you can't do that professionally," I said when the spell had broken and the unanimous applause in the little room died down.

"I don't like being on stage." He gulped the last of his Scotch.

"Why not?"

He shrugged. "Too public; too one-sided. Makes me uncomfortable. I like to see who's looking at me."

Me too. I didn't say it, but he heard it anyway. We were empathic, as they say, and I began to wonder if he was telepathic, the way he spoke my mind.

It was after midnight when Charlie and I said good night in the hallway outside our rooms. By then, sleep should have waited on the other side of my door and jumped out at me when I opened it. It wasn't even at home. Or maybe it was at home, my home, checked out of the hotel because of the poor service and the holidays and the fact that I wasn't paying any attention to it. Reminded me of Sally.

I settled in a chair next to the dresser in front of the bed. From here I could see both doors, the hall door, and the one to Charlie's room. The dresser protected me on the left, solid pressboard with two real drawers and two fake ones. It had no legs because it was bolted to the wall. The window was on my right, sealed against unconditioned night air and the noise of life six stories down. I was a rat trapped in a corner from which I could fight, but never escape. I sat and waited for morning.

I must have dozed because I dreamed. Charlie came through the connecting door, sat down at the dresser on my left, and played it. I did not recognize the song. He asked me what a musician looks like and I said a musician wears an orange mohawk. He grinned and disappeared. There was a scratching at the door. The bum from the parking garage came in, offering help. I declined, politely. He said if I did not shoot down the chopper his best friend would cut my throat and cry over my coffin. Then, Frank came in, hung his big picture over the window, and drew the curtains on it. Even Jello was in this dream, nailing boards over the doors, but before he finished, Frank shot him and slipped through to the hall, bolting the door behind him—to keep me safe, he said. Charlie's next-door neighbor, the one I kept forgetting and remembering, unbolted it and walked across the carpet toward me. I could not see his face clearly, but he still bothered me. It was in the way he walked. He opened his wallet and took out a picture of two people in front of a house in Iowa. I looked closely and recognized my wife and son.

I woke drenched in sweat, opened the curtains over the window, and stood with my forehead pressed to the cold glass, straining to see the street six stories below. Nothing moved. My eyes searched for movement along the walls of the skyscraper canyon in front of me. Nothing. I studied the buildings I could see, some taller than others, dotted with light and dark windows like random pattern checkerboards. I wondered if there might be a man standing in one of those windows, his forehead pressed against the glass, watching me. I imagined there was. I stepped back and closed the curtain. It seemed definitive. I felt relieved.

I did not expect to see Charlie again; he said he was leaving early on Christmas Eve. It was a surprise, then, to meet him in the rental car parking lot when I picked up the new car that morning. I gave him a lift around the airport circuit and dropped him off at the domestic terminal. He was flying back to Iowa to sell tractors. I drove to Edbrooke Avenue to see if Frank was still alive.

EIGHTEEN

On Christmas Eve morning, Jay and I stood next to my car in front of the pizza parlor on Edbrooke. Our stamping feet made the only sound in the frozen air, echoing down the street unanswered. We waited for, and I worried about, Frank. He was late.

I was miserable. This was the low point in this job for me. Other times would be bad, physically even worse, but this was plain misery. The uncertainty about Frank, about what the hell was going on. I was in a bad fifties horror movie, groping in a fog, knowing I'd end up as dinner for some shapeless monster rising out of the steaming muck in front of me any minute now. I was tired, to the point I thought I would die soon, hungry, and I had the shakes from too much coffee. And right then, I knew there was no other job for me.

The misery was almost part of the attraction. It was like early week in pilot training, when the flight commander would read an emergency scenario and study the faces of instructors and students in assorted stages of coffee high.

"What will you do, Lieutenant..." he would say, and every student would tense, waiting to hear his name. Sometimes it was my name. I would stand, the clock over my shoulder reading just after four a.m. A Styrofoam cup with an inch of cold coffee stood next to my open dash one, and I would pick up the book carefully so as not to spill the last bit of vile, black, necessary liquid. My mind would work. The right answer would come, and I could sit down. More than that, I could fly. For one more day, I could fly. Euphoria at dawn.

Frank's voice set the speed brakes on the memory. I landed back at Edbrooke.

"I'm still here," he said, "hale and hearty. No sign of a Mercedes. What about you?" He was asking me.

"Nothing. Maybe they've gone away."

"Not a chance. Maybe Mr. Turner can tell us where his buddies are lurking."

Jay scowled.

"What's your brief for today?" Frank asked him.

"I have no brief. I am released and at your service alone."

"When did that happen?"

"Last night."

"Did you see them?" asked Frank swinging his arms from front to back. It was cold that morning.

"Yes." There was a reluctant pause in Jay's voice. He was admitting compromise. I suppose I would pause, too.

"Well, how'd they look?" asked Frank. "Fresh, alert, and healthy?"

"No. Exhausted and rumpled."

"Poor dears." Frank clucked like a hen. "Did they happen to discuss their plans for me? Or maybe you already know their plans. Maybe it was a super-saver package deal, eh? Me and Hunsecker?"

"I did what I had to do to defend the Constitution of the United States." Jay poked his finger at Frank's chest. "You would have done the same in my shoes. You would if you had any balls."

"Sure, sure I would. I agree." Frank pushed Jay's hand away. "The only way to deal with incompetence is to snuff the incompetent. Good plan. Vladimir Ilyich and Uncle Joe would be proud. Which constitution did you say you were defending?"

"He was dirty, Frank," said Jay quietly. "I guarantee it."

Frank chuckled, stamped his feet, and looked at the sky.

"He was," insisted Jay. "Look. When have you known Charlemagne to work without verification?"

Frank's chin came down abruptly and he stared at Jay for a long minute. "Everybody makes mistakes. They're making one with me."

"I'm sorry to hear that," said Jay. "There was no mistake in Hunsecker's case and so far, you seem to be walking and talking all right. If there's anything I can do to help you stay that way, let me know. Charlemagne's jet landed at O'Hare this morning. Do you want me to put a hold on it?"

"No. Not yet." Frank turned to me. "You haven't left your new car alone, I hope?"

"No. It's right here." I pointed in front of me, then put my hand back in my pocket to prevent frostbite.

"Good. Let's go." Frank held up his hand in a signal to stop Jay from moving toward the car. "We'll see you later, Mr. Turner. Merry Christmas."

The two men stood in the cold in a long mutual glare. Jay broke the silence with what I thought was remarkable professional dignity. "You know how to reach me if you need me," he said. "Merry Christmas."

"You seem pretty cheerful this morning, Frank," I said after I started the car.

He did not answer me immediately because he was busy with the heater.

"Give it some gas, Steve. Let's get some heat in here."

"I said you're looking pretty cheerful, Frank. Why?"

"Head for 87th Street again," he said. Lukewarm air blew into the car. He adjusted the vent so it did not blow in his face. He fiddled with his seat and sat back with a sigh.

I gave up on an answer to my question.

"I am cheerful this morning, my brilliant lad," he said suddenly, "because, as Jay noticed, I am walking and talking, and the sun is shining—well, it is behind the clouds—and again like Jay said, Charlemagne rarely kills without verification. In my case, they aren't going to get verification, because there isn't any. By noon today, you and I will be winging our way home to Christmas dinner. Life is good. I feel good."

He sighed again and closed his eyes.

"You were happy and chipper before Jay said one word about verification." I pointed out. "Did you have sweet dreams or something?"

"I had a vision. Unfortunately, it was more of the nightmare variety. But I woke to two messages that made it all better."

"And what were they?"

"Answers to the two calls I made last night."

I waited. There was no point in pressing him, and the street demanded all my attention.

"The first message was from Alexandra Sobieski," he said. "I was pleased to learn that she is still alive."

"You called her?"

"I called a contact and have been rewarded with a message at my hotel this morning asking me to meet Alex at her father's house at nine o'clock. No doubt she's the one who brought the jet in. They must be getting ready to wind things up. You'd better step on it."

I did my best, but traffic was heavy.

"And the other message?" I asked.

"Was from Inch. He did what I told him to do, for a change. Of course, I had to use every dire threat in my vocabulary."

"You called Inch? The librarian? The man with the flaming sword who stands in the door of the vault guarding his precious documents from us infidels? You got him to do something for you?"

"I sure did." Frank was smug. "He's here and he brought the Charlemagne file. He also brought one of the heavy boys from the courier service to guard him and the file. I told him he could. He's such a nervous, suspicious little twit."

"That's magic, Frank. To get Inch to budge from his vault, on Christmas Eve, with a document, is just plain magic. I salute you." I saluted him and nearly hit the car in front of us.

"Just drive, Steve. I told Inch to meet us at Alex's father's house at nine-thirty. I'd like to have at least half an hour to talk to her first, so come on, step on it."

"I'm trying to. What are you planning to do with Inch's file?" I found a clear lane and made some progress.

"I'm going to give Alex those pictures."

I looked at him quickly. "Does Inch know that?"

"Of course not. I can't wait to see his face."

We had a good laugh at the thought.

Alexandra Sobieski was ordinary. I guess. She was in her early thirties, short, with glasses and curly brown hair. She wore a black suit with a straight skirt and black pumps. Absolutely ordinary, with an attraction, not beauty, that was equally absolutely compelling.

She sat in a corner of the living room of her late father's house, in the kind of chair that was popular in the sixties, hard, pseudo-modern, uncomfortable. Dust sheets had been piled in a corner, leaving a sofa and another chair uncovered. There was a cheerful fire in the fireplace, but otherwise the room was as ordinary as Alex.

Until then, I had confused the ordinary with the mediocre. Until then. Alexandra Sobieski was anything but mediocre.

Frank took a seat in the chair opposite Alex. I stood behind him by the front window, keeping a reluctant eye on our car parked on the street. There were two other men in the room, Alex's 'pilots' who would never have squeezed into the cockpit of a fighter. One stood a few feet to my left by the front door. He covered the front door. Literally. The other stood in the opening of a hallway that led to the rest of the house.

Frank expressed his sympathy. Alex told him to get on with it.

"Thank you for coming all this way on Christmas Eve," he said. He didn't seem willing to get on with it.

"We will not celebrate Christmas for two more weeks," said Alex. "I never could convince Misha's wife that it was Peter the Great, not God, who put Russia on the Julian calendar."

"She is Russian, then?" asked Frank.

"Was." Flat and hostile.

"I am sorry. When?"

"You know when. In October."

"Can you tell me anything?"

Frank shook his head as if to answer for her.

"Anything you want to know. My brief is easy."

It took Frank a while to get over the shock and form a question. While he rubbed his chin, Alex signaled the pilots to leave the room.

"Do you know anything about the operation?" asked Frank.

"Some."

"Was it commissioned or personal?"

"Both. I know very little about the commission, other than it was distasteful."

"But the personal?"

"Ask."

"Was it revenge?"

She nodded. "I know the story only second-hand, and it's an old one. Do you want to hear it?"

"Please."

"Misha came from a political family, not a specialist family like Vasily's. Misha's father was considered a nuisance in certain political circles. He angered quite a few people, mostly the extreme. When Misha was nineteen, the family drove to Vienna for a political convention. They made a holiday of it. It was Misha, his parents, his seventeen-year-old sister, and a six-year-old brother, in the car, with their chauffeur driving. They passed through a village where an ice cream vendor had a little cart on the street. Misha's little brother campaigned for an ice cream, and Misha got out of the car to buy one. As he paid the man, the car blew up behind him. The person who told me this worked in a bakery behind the ice cream cart. She said the heat from the flames melted the plastic umbrella on the cart. She also said that despite the noise of the fire, she could hear screaming from the car, even through the window of the shop, for almost a full minute after the explosion.

"Atrocities multiply themselves, I think. The person who bombed the car was a specialist named Jared. After the funeral—symbolic since there was almost nothing left—Louis and Misha went to Poland and pulled Vasily out of a prison. Vasily spent most of his adolescence in Polish jails, you see. The three of them paid Jared back the debt in vengeance—with interest. It was their first operation, not counting the prison break, and a complete success, if you want to call it that, except that one member of the Jared family, Eben, was in an English boarding school."

She stopped and looked at her hands in her lap.

"In January this year," she said, "a man named Slavin offered the team a commission on Eben Jared. Misha told him no. He was sure that Slavin was up to something. Besides, Vasily told me, Slavin's verification was useless.

"In July, Vasily drove to a city near our home for a business meeting. Our daughter begged him to let her go with him, but it was too dangerous. We said no. She disobeyed, as usual, and took her bicycle to follow him. I told Misha when I discovered her gone and he went after her. Mara caught up to her father in the parking lot of an office building. Right behind her was a man with a gun. Vasily pushed her out of the way. Misha's knife is very fast, but it was not fast enough this time. Vasily died in Mara's arms."

Alex closed her eyes and took a deep breath. She was grim, but dry-eyed when she looked again at Frank.

"Misha's son, Michael, came home from university and was allowed to help investigate. He was well trained for it." The sound of her voice scratched as though catching on painfully spicy food.

"During Vasily's funeral, Misha and I blamed each other every chance we had. Afterward, he came to my office with the most insufferably triumphant look on his face. He handed me a picture. He said Michael had found it in the apartment of the man who killed my husband. It was a picture of Mara, taken last Christmas, a picture I had given my father."

She looked at her hands, then at the fire, then at the ceiling, without fixing on anything. She rubbed her temples and I noticed her hands were shaking. "I won't tell you what that interview was like. I understand now that it is a serious crime to give a lonely old man a few pictures of his granddaughter." She said this loudly, with defiance.

"I thought my dad had burned them all," she said more quietly. "I had no idea any were missing, nor how many."

She put her face in her hands, dropped them, and stared at them in her lap.

"I had to tell Misha that there were other pictures, and that one would be valuable to the kind of person who would follow a little girl to shoot her father. I gave it to Papa because it was such a happy picture. I thought it would reassure him that his granddaughter was not growing up in a thieves' den."

She looked up at Frank. "I am sure you can imagine what I had to listen to when I warned Misha. I thought it was the worst day of my life. But it wasn't. In October, Misha and Louis were here, in Chicago, on Slavin's commission looking for that damned picture and trying to stop Jared."

She sighed and wiped at the corner of an eye with one fingertip. "Katya was my best friend, as sweet and mild as her husband is caustic and impossible. Nadia was fourteen. A pearl taken from a clam, and you should have seen her dance!"

Alex was crying freely now. She took out a white handkerchief. "We went to the ballet. That's all we did. Katya would not listen to Michael; none of us would listen to him. Nadia and Mara laughed and chattered as we left the theater and we did not even see the three men, but Michael did. He stopped two of them. The third one, a man with red hair, moved faster. Michael managed to pull Mara and me away from the building. I should be grateful and I am, but at the time I wished I had died with them. Vasily's death had always been anticipated. We lived with the possibility every day, but Katya and Nadia?" She shook her head and the tears dropped into her lap.

She looked at Frank. "Have I told you anything you didn't know?"

"You've told me more than I learned in fifteen years. Why?"

"Whoever gave Jared those pictures knew what he was doing. It wasn't one of ours. It had to be one of Jared's."

Frank stared at her. "It wasn't me."

"Verify, Frank."

"I will."

NINETEEN

Alex called one of the pilots from the other room. She unclipped the wire inside her lapel and handed it to him. "Take this out for a walk, will you please? It will be all right; he won't mind. I will take any blame for it. Just walk around the block and come back."

Once the ear and its bodyguard were gone, she turned to Frank. "It's my turn for an answer or two. I understand there was a child involved. Did they... is it... dead?"

"No," said Frank.

Alex drew a deep breath and closed her eyes. She opened them again and said, "When they left after the funeral, they were bent on revenge. Was it Michael who refused? You know, the young one, Misha's son. Did he refuse?"

"No. Mack said no."

"Mack! Misha?"

"Yes."

"He said no?"

"According to our information."

Frank stopped because Alex was not listening. Her head rested against the wall behind her, tears streaming from closed eyes. She opened them and smiled. "When I pray for a miracle, I always give God advice on how to go about it. I'm glad He never listens to me. His solutions are always better."

She sobered; the smile vanished. "But he is operational," she said to Frank. "Michael, I mean."

"Yes."

The pilot with the wire came in through the front door, and as I watched her pin it back on, it occurred to me that I had a question to ask. Something had puzzled me, and I was beginning to piece together an answer.

"Why wasn't Jer... Michael interested in Sarah?" I asked her from my spot by the window. Frank turned and popped his eyeballs in surprise. Alex's guarded reaction added weight to my private theory.

"I don't understand," she said. "Who is Sarah?"

I told her about the double date that was designed to gain access to Sarah's apartment. I watched her as I told her.

It had been bothering me since Sarah's first smile. She was not an easy woman to refuse. The operation made a liaison necessary; why was Michael unwilling? Reasons would have to be compelling. Like love or hate. Hate? Not likely. Sarah was one of the rare kinds of occupational hazards that make people think espionage is a good line to be in. Dottie was proof that things could always be worse.

Love, then. Was he attached, or infatuated, somewhere else?

Alex confirmed it. Her face turned red and she unconsciously covered her lips with her fingertips, as if to hide the memory of a kiss. She played with her wedding ring.

What would it be like to spend adolescence cloistered in the same house with this woman? She taught Michael flawless English. He must have been an eager learner. I would have been. And then a tragic early widowhood....

Michael went home unwilling to use Sara. He came back ready to woo Concordia, all reservations overcome, by death and revenge and....

"You turned him down then?" I asked Alex. "Why?"

The shock on her face answered for her. I never got a verbal reply.

Frank's reaction to my little deduction surprised me. I thought it was all pretty obvious. He twisted around in his seat and stared at me with frog-eyed wonder.

I shrugged. "Just wondering."

Inch came in shortly after that, protesting the rough treatment Alex's men gave his bodyguard as they pulled an unloaded .38 out of his belt. I don't know why people feel safer around empty guns. I don't.

Frank gave Inch a few choice threats, tailored to the whiney little bureaucrat's pressure points. It was a display of tradecraft that made me appreciate both the effectiveness of information as a weapon and the skill Frank possessed in wielding it. I learned a lot about my new job while watching the librarian squirm under the weight of three sentences.

Inch opened his briefcase and handed Frank a folder.

Alex stood by the fire. Frank walked up to her.

"I took two pictures," he admitted. "But I never gave them to Jared or anybody else. You're on the wrong track."

He opened the file and leafed through the loose sheets of paper. He flipped through them, first slowly, then quickly. There were no photos. I could see his profile in the glow from the fireplace. His frog eyes bulged in panic at the woman who seemed rather small and insignificant as she stood silently, grimly staring at him. The sweat on his bald head reflected the flames behind her. It had become suddenly very hot in the room.

Alex took the file from his hand and also leafed through it, while Inch protested feebly. He fell silent at a glance from Frank and only squeaked again once, helplessly, as Alex turned and dropped sheet after sheet into the fire.

"It wasn't me!" Frank squeezed the words through his teeth.

"Prove it," she said.

He spun around and faced Inch. "The logbook! Did you bring the log?"

"Of course," said Inch. "I always...."

"Just give it to me!" Frank snatched it from the briefcase before it was fully opened. He tore through the pages, searching for an entry.

Inch took it from him and found the right page almost immediately. "Twenty-first of June, and there's your signature."

"Not mine!"

Alex crossed the space silently and peered at the hand-written entries in Inch's book.

"It is your signature, Bud... uh, Frank," said Inch in a patient tone. "I'd recognize it anywhere."

"But you know it wasn't me. You had to have been there!"

"I wasn't there. I was on vacation that week. See?" Inch pointed at another column. "Pete Stanick, the new guy, checked you in."

"But Pete... Pete..." Frank was beginning to stammer.

"Pete died in that bad crash in Maryland on the Fourth of July, remember?" said Inch. "They said the fireworks caused it. I remember it because I have a very good memory for details. I've always thought I should be better utilized in the event of...."

Inch could not continue because Frank had him by the throat.

When Frank was calmer and could be released, he shook himself, straightened his tie, and faced the woman in the mourning suit. "I need two things from you, please," he said earnestly.

"Why should I?" she asked. "It's not as if we have access to a court of justice, is it? What gives you the right to an appellate review?"

"You should help me because you call yourself a Christian, and because I am innocent."

"Come off it, Frank. Nobody here is innocent."

"I'm innocent of this!" He put his hands out in front of him, flat, palms downward, as if to physically hold down his emotions. Calmed by force of will, he said, "This you'll understand—he'll understand. It's an incredible false flag. He's about to be conned. Tell him!"

"What are the two things you want from me?" she asked softly.

"Time and a miracle."

"How much time?"

"Twenty-four hours? Okay, six." No answer. "Two?"

"I'll try."

We left the little house off 87th Street with an uncertain grace period of two hours.

"What was all that about a miracle?" I asked as he got into the car. "Don't tell me she's devout."

"What?" Frank was distracted. "Depends on what you call devout."

"She's not then?" I asked, rather hoping, pointlessly in view of both our positions, that she wasn't.

"No. She is, really."

"But she is… was married to a specialist."

"So?" Frank challenged me with this word, and it alerted me to something in him. He stiffened and thrust out his chin, defending himself against attack. The subject meant something to him.

I took up the challenge. "So, the two are not compatible. It has to be one or the other."

Frank looked ahead, but I could see him studying me out of the corner of his eye. He nodded. "Maybe," he said. "But if you're one, then your business is with the other. The problem comes when your god tells you to kill."

"Huh?"

"Did you know that Barabbas was a terrorist?"

"He was?" This was my first ever Sunday school lesson. I didn't know who the hell Barabbas was, but I knew how to pretend.

"Yes, of course." Frank rubbed his hands in the cold. "Blew up Romans all the time." He waved at the steering wheel impatiently and told me to start the engine.

I didn't argue. I was on shaky ground anyway and maybe there was plastique in the old Roman empire. What did I know?

Frank watched my face carefully as I pulled out onto 87th Street, marking my grimace as the Mercedes swung in behind us.

He said, "I hope Alex comes through with that miracle."

TWENTY

We drove around, aimlessly, maybe in the general direction of Edbrooke Avenue, but not directly toward it. There had been no sign of the Mercedes for the last five minutes, but this was not reassuring.

"Where the hell are we going?" said Frank. "We should be heading for the airport. No. Not good. Too obvious. Come on Steve, get your brain in gear and help me, damn it! I have an escape hatch, but I need to get to it unnoticed. Think of a way to get me out of here."

"I...."

"You need to bail out in about an hour. So think quick."

"I'm not bailing out," I said. "Why are you giving up?"

Frank stared at me. He reminded me of Humpty Dumpty teetering on the wall. Round eyes in a round face full of concern. "The setup is perfect," he said calmly. "There are no holes in it. Even Pete Stanick is dead."

"Every possible witness is dead? What about Slavin?"

Frank dropped his chin and rolled his eyes up toward me, all patience and condescension. "First, tell me how you will find him and extract him in one hour. Then, explain how you will break him, and finally, maybe you can tell me how you plan to convince Mack that Slavin's word is worth anything."

"Okay. He's out. Jello?"

He gave me the same look and whistled softly.

"Fine. Fine. I see you're a pessimist, Frank. But I'm not giving up."

"Neither am I," he said. "I'm just getting out. I've seen Mack's work, lots of it, don't forget. What about a train?"

"What about Jared's people?"

"You may have noticed them in the morgue."

"His wife is still healthy."

"Healthy and happily ignorant of her husband's occupation."

"So she says."

Frank did not seem interested in the idea, so I dropped it. We did not speak again for several minutes. Frank stared blankly at the door handle. I glanced at him periodically but kept my attention fixed mostly on the traffic in front of me. The snow of the day before was gone from the street and piled on the curbs like a sculpture of a city skyline at dusk, all brown clumps and furrows.

"Frank, what about the little girl?" I turned the car east and headed for Edbrooke.

"Which little girl?" he asked sadly. "The little dead dancer?"

"No. Jared's little girl, Janey. She said she helped him, didn't she? Maybe she helped him on this case. Maybe she saw something. She's an incredible kid, maybe...."

"Maybe she planned the operation," said Frank sarcastically.

"We can ask," I said.

"We don't have time."

"We don't have time to do anything else."

"The apartment's not secure," he said as we pulled up in front of it. "You'll have to bring her down here."

Cordelia Jared came to the car with her daughter. That was fine with me. I was amazed she agreed to the interview at all. Frank did not look at them as they climbed into the back seat. I asked my questions from the front, half twisted so that I could see Janey seated behind Frank, but could only catch from the side the emanations of Cordelia's disgust for Me And My Kind.

We established that Jared often used his daughter to service dead drops and on two occasions as a live drop. The first time had been two years before. The second time was in the past June.

"You're sure it was June?" I sensed that I was on the right track.

"Yes," said the girl. "School was just out. It was June. It was hot, too. I remember because the guy had a suit on and I thought he looked hot. I wore shorts."

"The guy? What guy, Janey?"

"The guy who gave me the envelope for Daddy," she said with a look of *How dense can you be?*

"What did the guy look like?"

"Like a guy." She shrugged her shoulders.

"White guy? Black guy?"

"White."

"Tall? Short? Did he have a mustache?"

"No. He twitched. Besides that, he looked like anybody, I guess."

"He what?"

"He twitched. You know. His face went up and down on one side like he was winking but couldn't do it without moving the whole thing."

Frank turned around in his seat, trying to see the little genius directly behind him. Cordelia glared at him with the ferocity of a mother bear whose cub is threatened. I expected her to growl any second now.

"By any chance, did you look in the envelope, Janey?" I asked.

"Of course I did. Daddy wasn't angry about it, either. He said I should learn to look without making it obvious."

"What was in the envelope?" We could not waste any more time.

"Just some pictures."

"Pictures of what?" I closed my eyes, waiting for an answer that was taking eons too long.

"Pictures of some kids. And a lady."

My next question came from instinct, not conscious thought. "Did you recognize any of them, Janey?"

She did not answer right away but glanced at her mother. I twisted around in my seat to search Cordelia's face. She was puzzled.

"Did you recognize one of the kids?" I asked Janey again.

"Not then."

"But later?"

"Yes."

"Which one?"

"Jerry. One of them was Jerry." She said it quietly, head bowed.

Cordelia shook her head. "Why...why didn't you tell Daddy?"

"I didn't remember at first," said the little girl. "And when I did remember where I saw him before, I liked him too much. And Aunt Concordia liked him. I didn't want to spoil it for her." She sobbed. "I didn't know he was an enemy. I didn't know!"

"One more question," I said to the weeping child. Cordelia opened the car door. "Was this the man who gave you that envelope?" I pointed to Frank.

"No, of course not," said Janey. "He doesn't look like anybody. He looks like Mr. Douglas at the gas station."

...

"Right. Good work. No. Brilliant. I am truly brilliant," Frank said after Cordelia slammed the car door behind her.

"You!" I started the car as punctuation.

"That's right. I picked the right man for this job. I'm brilliant. Now then, my beamish boy, head for the airport. We have work to do, and when I say we...."

"I know. I know. You don't have a turd in your pocket."

"Nor a mouse. And I hope no other creatures are lurking in this car. You did follow the rules, I hope?"

"To the letter."

"Good. We have to call Alex and tell her where she'll find our star witness. Then we'll call the office and have them put Jello on ice."

"On ice?" I could not believe it. "You're not going to protect him! He nearly got you killed. Let them have him!"

"Like hell. They'll make a hero out of him. I want revenge. If Mack cuts his throat, I'll have to go to the funeral and say nice things about him to his relatives. I'll have to give a eulogy for the man who single-handedly destroyed more than fifteen years of my work. I want him to live. I want him to pay for his mistake."

"Mistake? Frank, you're fucking delusional. This was no mistake."

"Stop at the next phone booth you see," he said, ignoring me. "You followed all the rules? The car is secure?"

"All the rules."

"Nobody got near it?"

"Nobody." I was a little exasperated with his paranoia.

"Nobody's been in it?"

"Nobody. Except...."

"Except? Except who?"

I did not answer. I was thinking.

"It's impossible," I said when Frank began bouncing on the seat. "He's as American as apple pie."

"Who is?" Frank's eyes were bulging.

"Charlie."

"Who's Charlie?" He was sideways in his seat, leaning toward me, his eyes ahead of him by about a mile.

"This guy. I gave him a lift to the terminal this morning."

"In this car?"

Too many impressions crowded my memory at this point. I could not be sure which was real and which came from my dream the night before. I pulled the car over to the side of the road. Traffic roared by us. I heard Rachmaninov. A Santa Claus stood in front of a store on our right. I saw Charlie at the airport. Charlie in the hotel. Charlie in the bar. The Santa rang a bell. I heard Charlie talk about his father.

That was the trigger. I knew what it was that I was missing about Charlie's next-door neighbor. He reminded me of Charlie. It was in the walk, in the way he moved without seeming to. A silence of movement. And the people in Iowa? No resemblance. It was not just the difference in hair color, build, and facial lines. It was the difference in character. The people in that picture would not object to their son working for a tractor company. It was not exactly a fate worse than death in Iowa. Charlie the musician was not their son. He was Mack's son.

Frank saw it in my face and groped around under his seat. He found the device quickly and stared at it. "Bastards!" He rolled down his window and tossed it out, then leaned fully forward against the dashboard, beating his round, hairless head against it like Charlie Brown.

"You realize," he said to me through clenched teeth, "that they are, at this moment, positively rolling with laughter. The Frenchman has tears in his eyes, it's so funny."

There was nothing for me to say, but I said something stupid anyway, trying to draw attention away from my blunder. "There's a phone booth," I said, pointing ahead. "Did you want to call Alex?"

Frank was merciful. He said nothing. Keeping his head on the dash, he swiveled his face upward and looked at me.

"Right," I said. "No need. They know it wasn't you. What now?"

"Airport," he murmured.

I turned north and headed for O'Hare. For the first time since we came to Chicago, we were completely silent, which was odd, because it was also the first time nobody was listening.

TWENTY-ONE

I dragged my feet through the airport. Frank rolled on ahead of me. *Last one to the phones is a rotten egg.* I must have smelled pretty bad by then. Frank hollered over his shoulder as he moved at Mach through the main concourse, telling me to call Jay and put a hold on Charlemagne's airplane. Jay was not in. I left a message with somebody who didn't want to take messages on Christmas Eve. I calculated the chances of my message getting through and smiled.

I was not embarrassed. Well, okay. I did sting some from the thorough hoodwinking I had received from Charlie, or Jerry, or Michael, or whatever the hell his name is. But embarrassment did not make me drag my feet. I figured out that we were not only going to fail to protect Jello, but the mere attempt would irritate the team. Trying to bring Jello to justice would require us to share secrets, WEDGE secrets, talking about them openly, in a secret sort of way, in the black and even in the semi-black world, and none of that would go over big with Mack & Co.

I couldn't explain this to Frank when we traded results from the phone attempts. He was also unsuccessful. No one had seen Jello since he came back from the conference the day before. We dashed—he dashed, I dragged—through the terminal to the observation deck. We had no change for the viewing machines, having used it all on the phones. A business jet took off, but we could not see the tail number.

"You left a message?" Frank had a defeated look. "So did I."

After we returned the rental car and checked our bags, I talked Frank into having lunch while we waited for our flight home. We found a table in a dark corner of a large, empty restaurant in the terminal. Frank told me to order for him while he went to the toilet. I studied the menu, engrossed. After twenty-four hours without a full meal, I was ready for anything this place could offer.

"May I take your order, Suh?" said a scratchy voice over my right shoulder.

It was the exaggerated Southern accent in the "Suh" that started my mind working, but my mouth was already ordering a steak sandwich. When all the synapses had connected, and I knew the bum in the parking lot would not be working here as a waitress, I slammed the menu down in front of me, stood halfway, and stupidly thought about pulling my gun, though he had a good grip on my arm. I looked at him, hoping I might find a weakness, an opening, to strike and run.

The transformation was incredible. The Frenchman's dark, wavy hair was neatly cut, the temples slightly grey. He looked like a prosperous businessman. His beard was gone; he wore a three-piece suit, expensive and impeccable, and a gold watch. He laughed at me with black eyes and a full set of white teeth, then he made me move out of the choice corner seat I was in and set a dollar and some change on the table in front of me, a return on my investment in charity. I sat uncomfortably in another chair with my back to the door.

Charlie sat down next to him. He didn't introduce us. I felt the sting all over again, doubled now by the parking lot bum. Louis thought the whole thing hilarious. I wondered where Mack was. And Frank.

"We thought you were on your way to see Jello," I said nervously.

"He is not at home," said Louis. He leaned his chair back against the wall. He looked very casual.

Charlie was more tense.

I worried about Frank.

"Where is he?" I asked, more for something to say, and not really knowing which man I meant, Jello or Frank.

"He is in Chicago," answered Louis.

"Who?"

"Jello."

"Why?"

Louis did not answer and my mental effort to figure it out for myself was interrupted by the relief I had at the sight of Frank taking the chair on my right.

He was disheveled and subdued. The nap of the short fringe of hair circling his naturally tonsured head had been ruffled. His tie was crooked, the knot squeezed into a little ball at his throat. He played absently with a salt shaker. Whatever words were used in that men's room interview with a man he knew, or attempted to know, for more than fifteen years, they were not happy ones.

But he was alive.

Mack came in with him, also impeccable in a three-piece suit, the bulge of his SIG carefully masked by the cut of his coat. His hair was blond, like Charlie's, with no sign of grey, but his face was more lined. I found it hard to study him as he sat in the corner seat opposite me because he was so frankly dissecting me. His gaze was constant, hostile, penetrating, and it burned holes in me, making me squirm involuntarily.

Louis chuckled. "Brilliant bit of intelligence work with Alex there," he said to me. He looked at Charlie, smiling. "It raised our eyebrows, did it not, Michael?"

"Yeah. Thanks, Steve." Charlie's teeth were cemented together.

Louis' compliment was a great help, but it melted away under the blue-eyed inquisition from Mack. He recessed the silent torture long enough for us to order lunch from a laconic waitress, then leaned forward and began a verbal interrogation in German. I maintained my legend.

"Your German is abominable," he told me.

I had no answer. I was listening to his accent, trying to hear what had so frightened the Czech woman. I could not

tell. He spoke slowly; he sounded Austrian. He sounded ed-
ucated, upper class Austrian.

"How many children were on that airplane?" he asked,
boring blue holes in my brain.

Oh shit.

"What airplane?" I tried to look puzzled.

"The airplane you shot down over the Bering Sea."

"I don't know what you're talking about." I wanted to
vomit.

"Cut the crap, Steve," Charlie said in English. "No spy
verse spy games if you want to deal with us. Make your
choice right now."

I looked at Frank. His ping-pong ball eyes were fixed on
the salt shaker. No help there. I looked at Mack. The ice in
his blue eyes dazzled me. He raised his eyebrows slightly,
waiting for my decision. His expression seemed so hard, so
controlled, so alien to me, that I knew instinctively my answer did not matter to him at all. He would act on it, one
way or another, without another thought about it. The only
one to suffer any consequence or enjoy benefit from my next
words would be me.

"Seventeen," I said.

Frank rested his head on his hand and turned away from
me.

"And how many commissions are out against you?"
asked Mack.

"They're all petty two-bit contracts."

"How many?"

"Five that I know of."

"And your family?"

I swallowed. Hard. "All five are inclusive."

"Why are you here?"

Frank had said I would need a reason. I had one, even if it sounded hokey coming from me.

"I was trained as a warrior," I said. "I belong in battle."

"The battle against what?"

"Against the slaughter of innocents."

The waitress brought us food. We were silent as she put a plate in front of each of us. Jay came up without a sound, carrying an extra chair from another table. He put it between Louis and me and sat down on it, elbows on knees, head in his hands, breathing heavily. He had news.

"I found him," he said to Mack when the waitress cleared out.

Mack picked up his knife and fork.

"I found him," Jay went on, "and then I lost him." Each statement came in short bursts, like an SOS. "He met Slavin. Slavin had somebody else with him. Took us half an hour to figure out who it was."

Mack ate like a European, with both knife and upside-down fork. He chewed slowly. "Who?" he asked after swallowing.

"The Barracuda."

Jay expected some reaction. There was none from the team. Frank and I, on the other hand, choked on our French fries simultaneously. Jay took the opportunity to pinch three from my plate.

With Jared dead, The Barracuda became Slavin's top surviving solo specialist. He had a reputation for not being overly picky about his targets.

When my throat was clear and I could speak again, I asked, "Who's the target?"

Louis threw his head back in a long laugh, then leaned forward toward Frank. "How were you planning to prove to your bosses that Jello is dirty?" he asked him. "Where is your verification?"

At first, I did not see the connection. I did not understand that Louis was answering my question with a question. But the synapses connected again and I figured it out before Frank answered.

"I have three proofs," he said quietly to the salt shaker. "Steve Donovan, Cordelia Jared, and most important, Janey Jared."

"There is your answer," said Louis. "Not just one target. Three."

"They will take care of the easier ones first," Mack told Jay. He put down his knife and fork, wiped his mouth on a napkin, and set it beside his plate. "Have your watchers pick them up at Edbrooke, and this time, do not lose them. We will take our opportunity when The Barracuda finishes."

"I'll arrest him," said Jay.

"Fine," said Mack. "But Jello is mine."

A lot happened in the next few moments, but almost nothing was spoken aloud. A casual observer would not have understood it.

My decision should have surprised no one. Ideas confused me; Janey was real. I knew my action could endanger other equally real people in the future, but I counted on Frank's presence as a kind of insurance policy. I hoped he would have the good sense to fire me, but not until I woke from a nightmare in which a pretty little girl with a halo of soft brown hair lay in a cold room at the morgue, next drawer to her father.

My first decision was to rescue Janey myself, if I had to. This was obviously a last resort, since my chances of success made snow in the Sahara look like a sure bet. Janey's only real hope, as I saw it, was with the three men who had almost killed her two days before. My next decision, the one that probably impaired my ability to do my job—irreparably it seems—was to do whatever was necessary to commission an operation against The Barracuda. Within the next thirty seconds.

I looked at Frank. His expression was sympathetic, but he shook his head. "No authorization, Steve," he said.

That eliminated money as a motivator. My own meager resources were laughable; without the government, I had no hope of affording Charlemagne. I considered lying but rejected it on the grounds that I was not likely to be believed.

What about sympathy? Or altruism? I looked for some in Charlie. I couldn't tell. Like Mack, he was watching me, expressionless. I saw no sympathy there, and even less in Louis. His eyes held a hint of cruelty barely concealed. He would not volunteer to risk his life to save the daughter of a dead enemy. Mack would have to decide.

I looked at Jay last. In my last resort plan, I would need his support. He nodded. I could count on him. But I looked at him for another reason. I did not agree with what he had done, but at last I understood. I decided to offer the same as the price of a commission. I looked at Mack.

"For now," Mack said to me before I could speak, "it is enough that you are in our debt."

TWENTY-TWO

"So babysit," said the Frenchman. He waved the barrel of his gun at Sarah's apartment.

I was not sure why they brought me, but I knew it was a breach of the rules for me to be this close to an impending operation. I knocked softly on Sarah's door.

"Be very quiet and come with me," I said when she answered.

She looked surprised, but she complied. I held her arm firmly as we passed between Mack and Louis and walked to the stairway. Her smile was wasted on her former lover. He was busy picking the lock to the Jared apartment. Charlie was already heading through Sarah's flat to the kitchen window and the connecting fire escape.

"Do you have someplace to go?" I asked her as we stood in the doorway downstairs.

"My mother's, but...."

"Good. Do you have a car?" I had no time to enjoy her flirting. I was listening and watching.

"Yes." She pointed across the street.

An old Chevy was parked on Edbrooke, directly across from the pizza parlor. I walked her very quickly to it, opened the door, and shoved her into it.

"I don't have keys," she protested.

I hot-wired it.

"How will I...?"

"Just go. Now."

Instinctively, I stepped back into the shadowed doorway of a boarded-up grocery shop as she drove away. An alien movement caught my attention and made me take cover. It was alien because it did not belong in the place where I saw it, at the time that I saw it, on Christmas Eve. I stood in the shadows and peered across the street into the plate glass front of the pizza parlor. There was a tall shape at the telephone. Joshua Atkinson? Working, no doubt. Catching up after the pre-holiday rush or to prepare for the post-holiday rush. Why on the phone? Talking to his family. 'I'll be home by four o'clock. Tell the kids.' Did a man like Joshua Atkinson have a family? Why did his presence in his own place of business disturb me? Why did his phone call disturb me?

I waited and watched, disturbed.

My instinct was right. He came out of his shop in a manner I recognized. He did not want to be seen. He moved, he slunk, into position to check the east side of the Jared building. I could not see it, but I knew that Charlie should be up there. Was Atkinson acting as backup for Charlemagne? He ran across the intersection diagonally, crossing both streets at once and coming to the left, or west, of the apartment building, out of Charlie's view. He flattened himself against it. No. He was no backup. At least not for Charlemagne.

I pulled my weapon and followed quickly when he disappeared onto the roof of the lean-to at the back of the building. I stood precariously on the same trash can he had used to get up there, straining to hold myself by the elbows on the lowest point of the sloping corrugated plastic roof. There was no time to climb after Atkinson. He was at the other corner of the building, looking up, his gun pointing up toward the street, or toward Sarah's kitchen fire escape. He was ready to shoot.

I was in an awkward position and maybe should have taken greater care, but I did not know how much care Atkinson was taking. I only knew I had to fire before he did.

The bullet hit him in the right hip and spun him suddenly so that he dropped his weapon and slid down the sloping roof toward me. I should have been prepared for it, but the recoil from my weapon overbalanced me and I fell heavily onto my back, with the wind knocked out of me. I was not yet able to breathe when Atkinson launched himself at me from the roof eight feet above. I rolled away in time. He did not wait to catch his own breath before he attacked. His strength and size were superior to mine, but not his skill. I had only luck and better training. I used these.

I lost my gun, which was lucky, because I had been losing the battle for control of it. I gave a mighty heave when I saw the barrel pointing at my neck and felt the pressure of his hand on the finger I had on the trigger. The gun escaped both of us, flew against a trash can and discharged the round in the chamber. His other hand was closing around my throat and I had no way to dislodge it. My empty hand found a broken piece of concrete, flat with a sharp edge. I brought it up against his left temple. It was almost unnecessary; the unguided round from my gun had hit him just below the ribs and he could no longer breathe. He fell heavily, blue-tinged, bleeding and dying.

I looked up when I noticed the shadow. Charlie was standing on the lean-to roof, telling me to move. There was a suppressor on his Glock and my heart was pounding in my brain. I barely heard it as he put a bullet in Atkinson's head.

"Find your gun and get up here," Charlie said.

"The phone rang and things went sour," he continued as I scrambled back onto the trash can. "It's a stand-off. Papa against Slavin, Louis grinning at Jello and Jello quivering in a corner. Everybody's ready to shoot, but The Barracuda has his gun in the girl's ear. So it's up to me and here is what you're going to do."

"Me?"

He hoisted me to an unsteady stand on the roof. His strength was incredible.

"You said it's up to you," I babbled. "I can't...."

"Shut up." He pushed me diagonally up the roof. "Screw your rules. We're talking nanoseconds in timing here. The Barracuda's behind a microwave and some cabinets. I don't have anything lethal to shoot at, so you're going to help move him."

"I...."

"You're going to draw his fire. I'd do it, but he might hit me and that would ruin my aim."

"Hit?"

"Don't worry. He might miss."

"Might!"

"Listen, Steve," said Charlie. He shoved me up against the corner of the building. "Remember, you're on his list. You're a dead man anyway. Don't think we're going to stick around for your sake if the girl goes down."

I climbed the rusted fire escape ladder slowly, trying to be quiet and trying not to fall off.

"What about the mother?" I whispered over my shoulder.

"She's down. Be quiet."

I reached the third floor and crawled toward the front of the building. I cut my hand on broken glass below the Jareds' blown out kitchen window and looked inside from a bottom corner. I could see the Frenchman standing in the dining area off the kitchen, looking down into a far corner, smiling. A counter ran under the window and along a wall running perpendicular from it on the left. Cabinets were attached to the wall about eighteen inches above the counter. A small microwave stood at the end of it, maybe a dozen feet from me. I could see a shoulder in what looked like a tweed coat, between the top of the microwave and the bottom of the cabinet.

"Aim high," whispered Charlie. "But don't hit anything. Shoot at the top of the cabinet, then stay put so he has something to shoot at."

I looked at him. His expression was businesslike. He could have been a broker telling me to buy AT&T. I rose to my knees, faced into the window, and fired.

I heard three shots at almost the same moment. One was my unsuppressed Smith & Wesson booming across the tense stillness that had been. Next came two silenced shots: Charlie's next to my ear, and The Barracuda's. I should not have been able to hear that one, given the chaos of the moment, but I heard it distinctly, because it hit me.

I knew I was hit as I hung below the window, but that did not concern me as much as the possibility that Charlie might let go of my coat. He was not a lot better off. One arm was looped over the window sill; the other held me. The fire escape clanged as it settled in a jagged heap on the ground below us, kicking up a red dust. Through the noise and the ringing in my ears, I heard a man screaming, high pitched and sobbing but definitely male.

Louis and Mack pulled us in through the window. I lay panting on the kitchen counter for a few seconds, half strangled, my left arm strangely numb, until Mack yanked me off, set me on my feet and shoved me toward the dining room table. Under the table, Louis crouched over the still form of Cordelia Jared. Janey sat by her mother's side, holding her hand, rocking and sobbing with an increasing intensity that was growing into hysteria. Already, her cries were replacing the noise from Jello, bruised and bleeding in a corner of the living room. His screams were now mere whimpers.

"Babysit," ordered Mack, shoving me toward the group under the table.

"Tell her," Louis said in German, "that her mother is alive, but she must not move her. Tell her to hold her hand until the ambulance comes. It will be here soon. You stay with her."

Charlie gave me a series of instructions about a commuter flight to Detroit out of Midway airport in the morning. I absorbed his instructions passively, without understanding them, distracted by the crescendo of Janey's screams.

Mack shoved me again, roughly, so that, though he struck the back of my left shoulder, I felt a searing pain in the front, on the side of my neck, bringing me back to an even more painful awareness of everything that was going on. I envied Cordelia her unconscious oblivion.

"Do something about the girl!" Mack shouted at me.

I looked down at Janey. She was now out of control.

Charlie pointed at Jello and said to Mack, "What about him?"

I knelt by Janey and took her in my arms, muttering something soothing. My grip on her was enough to prevent physical damage, but I failed to stop her from seeing Jello die, and I regret that because he died badly when Mack cut him. I don't know why. He should have slumped quietly, but instead, he threw his arms up and his legs out, flailing at the air and spewing blood with a look of horror on his face. I held Janey screaming and I wanted to scream with her. But I told her not to look and turned her face away.

We waited for the ambulance no more than five minutes though it seemed longer, and Janey was calm during the last part of it. We waited in the silence and smell of spent gunfire, spilled blood, and satiated rage.

But what pierced me through more than worry, sorrow, and pain, all of which I felt then, was the knowledge—not the intellectual kind stored in a few brain cells but knowledge organic, permeating every part of me—the knowledge that the hatred in that room would not be buried with the corpses that waited with us.

TWENTY-THREE

J ay met me in the ambulance and gave me a shopping bag
with some things in it. Christmas gifts, he said, and a
message to please deliver them. I spent the night in a windowless closet of a room at Roseland Community Hospital,
contemplating the gifts, unwrapped and without addresses
or explanation. *Another fucking test*, I thought wearily. Another logic puzzle. But despite the pain, I was comfortable
and the puzzle helped to pass the time until my watcher fell
asleep and I could get out shortly before dawn.

I found Janey in another closet-room near the intensive
care unit. She was calm, in an adult way, with a maturity
that frightened me. Her eyes were badly swollen from crying
and her soft brown hair was matted in a wild series of flat-
nesses ranged about her head like fields on a terraced moun-
tainside. She told me with a hopeful note in her voice that

her mother was expected to live, but the music in her tone was flattened, and the hope had a tinny ring to it.

She gazed at the object I held out to her for a long time before looking into my face incredulously.

"You expect me to accept that from him?"

I shrugged. I didn't know what I expected.

"Jerry's my enemy," she said flatly. "He is the worst kind of enemy. He pretended to be my friend."

I was tempted to remind her that it was Jerry who shot The Barracuda, but it occurred to me she might not consider that such a very great favor right now.

She looked again at the gift in my hand. I looked down at it too, searching for something to say. It was an exquisite little music box. I turned the key, and a porcelain ballerina, slender and wearing a tutu, turned in a slow pirouette on a crystal stage.

I looked at Janey, and as if to fill a pause in an ordinary conversation, I said, "His sister was a dancer, you know."

She stared at me for a long time, and I watched her piece everything together silently. I could see her understanding grow and her expression change. It did not comfort me but only frightened me more because I thought she was far too young to share such a history. She took the box from my hand.

"Tell him thank you," she said to me with a steady eye. "But I know we are still enemies."

Then she dismissed me. Without word or gesture, she shut me out. I knew it and accepted it because she was no little girl on the edge of adolescence. She was a product of centuries.

...

I found Sarah at the address she had slipped to me as I shoved her into her car. Her mother answered the door with the same smile, bestowing it on me with equal generosity. Sarah joined in until I was surrounded by smiles. They were happy to see me.

They invited me in. A tin tree in a corner supported a few blue and white bulbs. Christmas cards proclaimed "Season's Greetings" from a table surrounded by a sectional sofa in black vinyl. I was invited to sit down. I declined.

Sarah enthusiastically accepted the bottle of expensive and unpronounceable French perfume I gave her from Louis. It was one of those rare occasions when it's good to be the messenger. She acted as though the gift came from me.

Her mother offered me coffee. I declined again. I desperately wanted a cup of coffee that morning, but the pain around my neck was getting worse and I had to catch a flight. I disentangled myself from Sarah's affection and shifted my left arm painfully in its sling. This only increased their concern, and their sympathy, and their attempts to comfort me, but I fought hard and managed to get out of there with my virtue intact.

...

There was a sad grey light over the city by seven that morning when I approached the little house behind the gas station and entered the backyard from an alley. The miniature clouds I produced by breathing seemed to be the only things hinting at life in the still neighborhood, but when I stood before the back door, I felt a difference here. I heard squeals of laughter in little voices, pans rattling in the kitchen, slippers on the kitchen floor. I knocked.

The door opened. Samantha's face changed as quickly as did comments and questions—delight, concern, confusion. She invited me in.

A small child ran into the kitchen in Mickey Mouse slippers and Batman pajamas. "Look, Gamma!" he said, holding up a toy space shuttle. "Look what I got!"

"Now didn't I ask you to wait until I come back?" She opened the oven door. "I'll be right there. Tell everybody to be patient."

She basted an enormous turkey that was already filling the house with the smell of sage and onions. She closed the oven door, poured coffee in a mug, and stuffed the mug into my good hand, not listening to my polite refusal. It was hot and delicious and very needed, but I spilled a few drops on the spotless linoleum floor as Samantha pulled me by the sleeve into the living room.

"Everybody! Look who's here!" she shouted over the din.

I was cheered at as if I were Santa himself by people who had never seen me before. They cleared away torn wrappings and ribbons from a place on the sofa and directed me to it. It took fifteen minutes for George to introduce me to those of his children and their families who had come from out of town. Samantha elaborated each introduction, so that I knew most of each family's history by the time she was finished. The local children would come later that afternoon, she told me. I wondered how they would all fit in that little house. The room was very full already. The unwrapping had begun again in earnest as soon as Samantha came into the room and continued through the introductions, punctuating them with excited squeals.

I took the little box out of my pocket and gave it to Sam. George looked over her shoulder as she opened it. She took out a small cross of diamonds on a fine gold chain. Her husband helped her with the clasp.

She beamed at me with tears in her eyes. "From Mack?"

I nodded.

"You've seen him? How is he?" asked George.

I did not know what to say. Obviously, these people knew him differently than I did. I shut out the memory of the killer I had seen in action the previous afternoon and remembered instead the cold, hostile man I had met in an airport restaurant. That was no help.

"Tired," is how I answered George.

It was not easy to refuse their invitation to dinner. The house was comfortable and warm. There was something delicious announcing itself from the kitchen. The people were friendly and interesting and their children delightful. But I had my own to go to and I was becoming impatient to get there. As I said goodbye to everyone and walked back to the kitchen with George and Samantha, I understood what it was that Mack had found here at a time when he no longer had his own. This was a world in which every face was a window to a human soul. It must have saved his life. It certainly saved the lives of others.

I remembered one of those others sitting alone in a little room at Roseland Hospital. I told them about Janey and gave them Jay Turner's number to arrange something. As I stood with my hand on the kitchen door, George gave Sam one of his significant 'leave us' looks which I was just beginning to recognize, and turned to me.

"I saw you, you know," he began quietly. "I heard a gunshot and I ran over to see what I could do. I watched you two up there, you and Mack's kid, saw you fall. I was trying to figure out a way to help when the other two pulled you in. I didn't realize you were one of them when you came here the other day."

You can't keep your hands clean if you dig in the dirt. Even if you use a shovel.

I said to George, "I'm not one of them."

He answered me with a look that asked my own question. *What are you then?*

I pondered this on the flight home. *Unemployed* was the first answer I came up with.

...

An artsy-crafty wreath decorated my front door. The mini-van was parked on the street and needed washing. My wife met me as soon as I cleared the wreath. I kissed her, held her, and buried my face for a minute in the brown hair that fell to her shoulders in soft ringlet curls. She led me to the sofa and took the shopping bag with the last gift still in it. This consti-tuted my luggage, since everything else had been checked onto another flight at O'Hare the day before.

The solution to the last puzzle from Charlemagne elud-ed me and I brought it home thinking I'd return it through Frank. It was a pen and stationery set, obviously for a woman, but I had no clue as to which woman. The pen was expensive, chrome with gold trim, very feminine. The paper was also expensive, but it was the pattern around the border that threw me.

It didn't fit any of the women I had met. It was too young for the old Czech lady, and anyway, there was only fear in that relationship. It was too pink and bourgeois for Cordelia Jared. The design was one of those pseudo-country designs with rocking horses done in pink, white and blue, like the rocking horses we had all over our kitchen. It was just the sort of thing my wife would like, I realized, as a frost took a grip on my heart.

I collapsed on the sofa without even asking about my son. Two inches of snow lay on the lawn reflecting the light of a sunny December day over my shoulder through the open curtains behind me. My wife sat next to me and took the stationery set out of the bag.

"How nice," she said.

"No," I said in muted panic. "It's not for you."

"Yes, it is." She opened the box and took out the item that had puzzled me most. It was a small plastic envelope holding a folded piece of carbon paper, business sized, larger than the stationery.

"And this is for you." She handed me the envelope.

Sometimes it is impossible to move in a nightmare.

"They came the day you left," she said carefully. "They were charming. They said they knew you. We had coffee. They said you were waiting for a flight to Chicago and they would be on it with you, but they promised you would be home for Christmas. I knew I shouldn't have let them in when they took off their coats and I saw all the guns. And the one, Michael's father, he really frightens me." She looked down at the box on her lap, then up at me again, biting her lower lip.

I was still speechless.

"They explained a lot," she continued. "They said I had a need to know because it affects me. I'll say it does." There was accusation in her voice.

"The tallest one was unhappy with the locks on the doors and windows," she said. "He put new ones in and said to tell you not to change them. There are no devices in them, he said. There are devices you won't find, but they're not in the locks, so keep them. These are necessary. He said the new locks won't stop him, but they will stop most." She glanced at the playpen in the corner where our son slept.

"Sally...."

"Be quiet and listen," she interrupted. "This is important. I am to tell you that the rules are changed and from now on you follow their rules. Michael said they would prefer no more files, period, but they know this is unrealistic in a bureaucracy. So they decided on a compromise. They want to be on the mailing list."

She paused to see if I understood. I nodded. "He asked me for a picture of us." She paused again when she saw the alarm on my face. "I gave him one. Michael's father said to tell you that he now has a file on you. Anything you write, anything you find, anything you feel you have an urge to steal, needs to be in it."

I stood up and looked at the living room of my home on Christmas Day. The tree was the same, decorated with wreaths and geese saying 'welcome'. The clock on the piano ticked. The sofa was flowery, overstuffed and comfortable. I could smell a turkey like Samantha's, with sage and onions. But for once, I was not hungry.

I walked to the window. There was a new lock on it. Outside I had a picture-perfect view of middle America, safe suburbia. I wanted, briefly, to return to it, but it was only a painting with no space in it for me. I had been painted out. I closed the curtains.

TWENTY-FOUR

F rank gave Jello's eulogy. He said nice things about him, did his gagging privately. It was too secret, they decided, or it was too embarrassing, to publish the truth, and so, for the sake of the family, for the sake of the Section, for the sake of…. Jello's coffin had a flag on it. Frank almost walked out when he saw it. A few of us put on a military display of honorably removing and folding it for Jello's widow. Nobody seemed to notice we were a few hours early. Then we marched Frank up to the pulpit where he delivered a few diluted platitudes with a taut smile. Some people thought the occasional choking in his voice was evidence of how attached he had been to his fallen comrade. Several colleagues told him this, and when he choked again at the word comrade, they took it as proof that no amount of bureaucratic wrangling could come between true friends.

Friendship was a sore topic with Frank after Jello's death because he knew he had lost his friendship with Mack, lost it before he knew he had it. I still don't know what was said in that men's room at O'Hare airport, but it was probably the first time those two ever spoke an honest word to each other in a decade and a half. How they had developed an affection for each other is beyond me, but I am convinced it was this that kept Frank alive when all the evidence was against him.

Frank did not forget my part in Alex's miracle. Maybe as a reaction against the possibility of failing another friend, he stuck by me during the ordeal of the following months.

The aftershocks of Jello's betrayal registered quite a few points on the Section scale. Damage assessment was constant and penetrating. There was even talk about alerting the FBI concerning Jay Turner. This idea was quashed at a higher level, though, where interagency cooperation is unfashionable.

After investigation came retribution, vindictive and indiscriminate. I was an early victim. The board decided that I killed Joshua Atkinson who was, they discovered, a sleeper agent recruited by the KGB in Cambodia and activated for this operation. They decided I killed him because they found an extra bullet of mine lodged in a beam of the lean-to. From this, they deduced that the round that hit his heart was no accident. I don't know how that extra bullet got there. They insisted Charlie's round was not the cause of death. I had to acknowledge that I broke a few rules, and I suppose I was not very cooperative during the polygraph. Anyway, I was sacked.

Almost.

Frank went out on a limb from his new exalted position in the late Jello's office and reminded them of the need for verification. The board tried to contact the only witness to Atkinson's death, the one whose bullet they said could not have killed him. They could not contact him. Frank tried. He failed, too. They asked me to try and as luck would have it, I managed to set up a meeting in a hotel room in Berne.

The main result of that meeting was my retention as an employee and as Charlemagne's American babysitter. I kept my new job, but along with it I took on what seems to be an indelible stigma of suspicion. I became a leper.

Sometimes it can be funny, as it was when I heard two rookies whispering about me by the coffee machine. I popped out at them from around the corner, and they disappeared down the corridor in a flash, leaving me a hot cup of coffee in the machine. Free.

Most of the time, though, my reputation is a disability that threatens my effectiveness. Frank tells me not to worry. He says it was the same when he started. It will wear off, he says.

I wish I could be so sure, but I see too many differences between Frank and me to count on my career following his. One example is my relationship with Charlie. We use the familiar form, *du*, with each other. Mack and Frank never used anything but the formal, *Sie*.

I think the biggest difference between us was implied by Mack during that meeting in Berne. There were six of us in the room, drinking a bottle of Charlie's scotch. I was sorry to see that Frank and Mack did not speak to each other. The chairman of the board that was sacking me asked them about a dozen unnecessary questions, all of them ignored with icy stares. Charlie was a singularly uncooperative witness.

Exasperated, the chairman said finally, "Why did you agree to this meeting?"

"Steve requested it," Charlie said with a shrug.

"Is Donovan the only one who can request a meeting with you?"

Charlie nodded and poured a little more into my glass.

"Why?" The chairman was warming up now that he was getting a few responses.

Mack answered. He leaned back in his chair, relaxed, but still caustic. He smiled half way, maybe from the scotch, or from the joke Louis had just told him in French. Anyway, it was at least half a smile, but it disappeared when he answered the chairman.

"When the Allies liberated Dachau," he said, "they were so appalled at what they saw, that they shot the camp guards on the spot."

The chairman wrinkled his brow, trying to take this in.

"They broke the rules," said Mack.

"Who?" asked the chairman. "The camp guards or the Allies?"

"The Allies. They killed their prisoners. The men they killed had obeyed their orders by killing their prisoners."

Frank and I looked at each other in surprise. This was a virtual flood from a man who usually kept his words to himself.

"I don't understand." At least the chairman was honest.

Maybe that was why Mack explained more without sounding irritated. "Bureaucracies depend on men who follow the rules. Controlling a bureaucracy depends on men who know when to break them."

"But breaking the rules can go too far." The chairman shifted in his chair. "It can be disastrous."

This time Louis spoke. "Yes. It requires the ultimate risk, the risk of being wrong."

"We have many men besides Donovan," insisted the chairman, "who are Allies, not camp guards, who are capable of taking that risk."

"Perhaps," said Mack. He looked at the scotch in his glass.

"Will you be willing to work with one of them?"

"No."

"Only Donovan is acceptable?"

"Yes."

"Why?"

Mack leaned forward and looked at me while he answered. Frank said later it was a threat, but I knew better.

"Because he lives where we do," Mack said to the chair-man as he looked into, not at, me.

"Where is that?"

Mack raised his glass to me slightly—a toast. "I believe Frank calls it a room without doors."

[cc: WEDGE]

EPILOGUE

The tall man was the kind who always got promoted. He had a manufactured face, except for horsey nostrils and lots of hair that greyed correctly at the temples, inspiring confidence in the wisdom of his years, until he opened his mouth.

"Are you Leo Vilseck?" He pronounced it 'vile sack.'

Leo nodded. "Yes, Sir."

The man wrinkled his horsey nose and looked at the file in front of him.

"This document refers to a Frank Cardova. Who is he?"

"That's me, Sir. I am Frank Cardova. It's my game name. Vilseck is my real name." He pronounced it properly, not being sufficiently subservient to mispronounce his own name.

"Game name?" The man was truly lost now. The other two bureaucrats on the investigative panel leaned in to him from either side. They advised. They explained a little, too. Only a very little. He favored Frank Leo Cardova Vile-Sack with a solemn look, as befits the chairman of a panel, to disguise the fact that he didn't know beans.

He knew so little, in fact, that he was unaware that Frank had pegged precisely how ignorant he was.

"We are here today, Mr. Cardova, to discuss the recent defection of your subordinate, one Stephen Donovan." He looked at the paper again. "And another subordinate, Daniel

Martin Kessler." His nose drew up toward his eyebrows. The bureaucrat to his left whispered to him. "They're what? The same man?" He looked up at Frank-Leo. "Do you have anything to say?"

"He hasn't defected, Sir. He just quit."

The bureaucrat on the chairman's right interrupted. "He joined his own team, Buddy. That's a defection."

"Who is Buddy?" asked the chairman.

"Look, Bruno," said Frank, "Steve is free to quit his job any time. It's the American way."

"Are you Bruno?" The chairman looked to his right. "I thought you were Thomas Stevenson?"

"He can't quit and then carry all his secrets across to his team," said Bruno.

"All his secrets were about the team. Which one do you think will surprise Charlemagne?" Frank's bulging eyes threatened to leap out at them.

"Charlene? Is there a woman involved in this?" The chairman searched the paper on the table.

"There are sensitive sources and methods," stammered Bruno.

"Come off it, Bruno," said Frank. "You met them in Berne. What methods do you think Steve could use that Mack wouldn't know about anyway?"

Bruno shuddered.

The chairman searched for some mention of Max.

The man to his left spoke. "I'd just like to know why, Buddy. Can you tell us that?"

"You know why, Gizmo. The third attempt, when his wife's car blew up and the neighbor's cat died under it— their sixth new neighbor in two months—and the baby almost toddled right into the flames trying to save that cat. That's what did it. He didn't have a choice. He has to protect them somehow."

The chairman put his hand to his forehead. "Gizmo?" he muttered.

"You think Charlemagne did it?"

"Of course not, Giz, you bonehead. Steve's got enough enemies of his own to more than qualify him for the team. He's where he belongs. I should have seen it coming long ago."

The chairman tried to regain control. "We must assess the damage, determine what information has been compromised, initiate corrective action, institute legal action."

"Nothing's been compromised," Frank said flatly.

The chairman looked up from the paper he was reading. "Nothing?"

"Nothing." Frank swung his round head from side to side.

The chairman looked at Gizmo, who covered his upper lip with his lower lip and shrugged. Bruno sighed and pushed back his chair.

"In that case, I find no cause for further action." The chairman closed the file. He noticed for the first time that the cover was striped diagonally with strips of red tape, and in between the strips, a name was printed in bold letters. "Now who," he groaned, "is WEDGE?"

The End

Will Steve be able to keep his job? His marriage? His life? Find out in the next Charlemagne file, Brevet Wedge, available at your favorite store by going to: https://books2read.com/u/4NgKXx

Join the Charlemagne Files newsletter for more stories and information about the series, its world of covert operations, and the lives of the characters on the team. Join here: https://www.charlemagnefiles.com/contact

If you enjoyed this book, please leave a short review at your favorite bookstore.

CHARLEMAGNE AND THE SECTION

The fictional world of The Section follows a few conventions. It may help the first-time reader of The Charlemagne Files to know some of these.

Who/what/ where is The Section?

The Section is a department of an intelligence agency of the United States. Its employees are civil servants. It includes support staff members who provide identity documents, financial controls, and physical and document security. The offices are near the East Coast, maybe Virginia.

The operational agents are called babysitters. They arrange on-site logistical support for freelance specialists during operations. Most operations are not conducted within the United States, with some exceptions.

Babysitters themselves do not carry identity documents in their names during an operation and never carry any official identification from their organization. Their purpose is to allow the organization to deny any association with them or their mission.

Nicknames

Babysitters in The Section receive nicknames from their coworkers when they join the office. These names are often undesirable and used mercilessly among the members of the office. It is part of the team-building process in a stressful occupation.

Coins

Challenge coins are traditionally stamped with symbols or mottos that designate the intelligence unit of their owners. The tradition is that when members of the unit are present at the bar and one produces his coin, all must produce theirs. Anyone failing to show their coin is responsible for the bar tab. If all produce their coins, then the challenger who first produced his or her coin is responsible for the tab.

File designations

The highest classification of information is Top Secret. Beyond Top Secret, more sensitive information is strictly controlled in a number of ways including designation as Sensitive Compartmented Information (SCI). This requires an additional clearance and often a named clearance based on Need-To-Know.

In The Section, files on specialists or specialist teams receive a one-word code name, printed across the file and restricted to very few people. When a solo or specialist team is employed on an operation, another designator word will refer to the operation and will be used for funding, reports, etc.

The Section's file name for Charlemagne is WEDGE. Thus CETUS WEDGE (second book of the Charlemagne Files) means an operation dubbed CETUS using the team called WEDGE.

Specialist

A team or solo operative used by Western governments for black operations conducted without fingerprints in high-risk situations expected to involve death.

GLOSSARY OF USEFUL TERMS (GUT)

AC - Aircraft Commander. The pilot who flies from the left seat of the cockpit and is in command of the aircraft, its crew, and any passengers.

AGE - Aircraft Ground Equipment. Air Force term for what is sometimes called ground support equipment in civilian contexts. Includes things like ground power units, air start units, dollies, jacks, lights, tugs, and tractors.

AFSC - Air Force Specialty Code, also called a career field in casual conversation. Designated by an alpha-numeric code that identifies a person's specific job and skill level.

Babysitter - term devised by the author to indicate those who provide logistic cover and support to the more dangerous operatives.

Bear - NATO name for the Russian TU-95, a strategic bomber used by the Soviets for reconnaissance missions at or over the boundaries of US airspace. Fighters, especially those from Alaskan or coastal bases, intercepted these forays regularly, a mutual game played by US reconnaissance platforms and MIG fighters near Soviet airspace.

Bring-Up Investigation: An expansion of a security investigation to add information because of a time-lapse, usually five years, since the last investigation, or to require addition-al details for a higher level of clearance.

Class B's - (Air Force) Blue uniform with shirt and tie but not the more formal blue coat.

Class B bachelor - person on temporary duty away from his/her home unit who removes his or her wedding ring for reasons not having to do with safety around the aircraft.

Cockroaches in the car - Okinawa's climate is hot and quite humid. Americans stationed there often buy their cars very used, somewhat rusty, and if not already home to the local insect wildlife, eventually infested. It is advisable at night to shoo them off the seat before sitting down.

COMSEC - Communications Security.

HUMINT - Human Intelligence. Not a comment on the thinking power of Homo sapiens. This refers to the gathering of information and leverage through the use of human relations, manipulations, and interactions.

Kadena Air Base - Large U.S. Air Force base on Okinawa, Japan. Known as the Keystone of the Pacific, it is home to the 18th Wing. Twenty thousand military members and federal employees and their dependents live or work on the base.

Making regular - Only graduates of the Air Force Academy are commissioned as regular officers when they become second lieutenants. All others, such as ROTC and OTS graduates, are commissioned as reserve officers even though they are on full-time active duty. Approximately four years later, a promotion board decides whether such officers should be offered regular commissions, usually when they pin on captain. It is the first real mark of successful career progression for a non-academy grad, though nothing tangible goes with it. One's boss knows one made it, and that means everything.

MREs - meals, ready to eat. Modern successors to K-rations and other attempts at field rations.

O-6 - A full colonel, as opposed to a lieutenant colonel. Also popularly referred to as a full bird colonel, because of the eagle insignia of rank.

Okuma Military Resort, Okinawa - Beach resort on Okinawa for use by armed forces personnel, federal employees, and their dependents.

Q - colloquial term for the BOQ or VOQ, bachelor officer quarters (for permanent duty) or visiting officer quarters (for those on temporary duty).

Škorpion - Czech-made submachine pistol.

Skoshi KOOM - Iconic restaurant on Kadena Air Base, now called Jack's Place after the man who made it the favorite haunt of so many, including the author. Skoshi is Japanese for small and KOOM stands for Kadena Officers' Open Mess.

Squadron Officer School - a military education course for company-grade officers (lieutenants and captains) held at Maxwell AFB, Montgomery, AL. At the time of Captain Nolan's attendance, it would have been 12 weeks long. Selection for in-residence attendance was somewhat competitive.

Tanker - An aircraft that refuels other airplanes in flight. A tanker of the 909th Air Refueling Squadron is a Boeing 707 designated as the KC-135. At the time of this story, the crew of a 135 included the aircraft commander, co-pilot, navigator, and boom operator.

TDY - Temporary duty, usually requiring travel away from one's permanent duty station.

UCMJ - Uniform Code of Military Justice - legal foundation of military conduct. All military members are subject to its jurisdiction, regardless of their location.

Zoomie - Graduate of the United States Air Force Academy

GLOSSARY OF GAME NAMES

Frank Cardova: long-time babysitter of Charlemagne; later, head of The Section; his real name is Leo Vilseck; Section nickname is Buddy.

Jay Turner: FBI counterintelligence agent with a private agenda; no aliases.

Mack: so dubbed by Western babysitters because he uses a knife at times; leader and decision maker of Charlemagne; called Misha by other members of his team; probable real name is Michael; last name is unknown.

The Frenchman: marksman and technical expert of Charlemagne; real name is Louis; last name unknown.

Vasily Sobieski: deceased explosives expert and martial artist whose father was a noted solo specialist; no aliases.

Charlie Taylor: marksman; son of Mack; probable real name is Michael; last name unknown.

Steve Donovan: recent new member of Charlemagne; martial artist; former fighter pilot; abandoned real name was Daniel Martin Kessler.

www.ingramcontent.com/pod-product-compliance
Lightning Source LLC
Chambersburg PA
CBHW060546260626
47161CB00003B/1082